MY BESTIES

THE COME UP

A NOVEL

ASIA HILL

GOOD 2 GO PUBLICATIONS

ISBN: 9780990869450

Published 2015 by Good2Go Publishing
7311 W. Glass Lane, Laveen, AZ 85339
www.good2gopublishing.com
Twitter @good2gobooks
G2G@good2gopublishing.com
Facebook.com/good2gopublishing
ThirdLane Marketing: Brian James
Brian@good2gopublishing.com

Cover Design: Davida Baldwin

Printed in the United States of America

Acknowledgments

All praise is due to Allah. Without his presence in my life, I wouldn't be here today.

Jae'lyn, Jacob, and Ja'taya. I am in love with the thought of loving you. My drive and my struggle is all for you. Mommy loves you wholeheartedly.

To my parents, Maria and Albert, I could never take back the pain I have caused you over the years. I am truly sorry!

Thank you for never leaving my side, and thank you for loving me, even when I was not loveable.

Maria George, you are the best sister I never had. You loved me when I gave up on loving myself. Thank you for being who you said you were.... Real!

Lindell Blount, thank you for showing me what a real man is. We started from the bottom and now we're here! Let's get it!

Miranda Dixon, girl, girl, girl you are something else. I love you for being my good in all of this bad.no matter what we go through I'm not going nowhere. Thank you for showing me that I was worth it.

I hope you know that you are worth it too. Thank you for loving me!

Good2go publishing, thank you for giving me the chance to join a winning team! Now let's win.

Last but certainly not least, I dedicate this book to my Uncle Aaron house. Losing you was a hard pill to swallow. I'll love you forever. This is for you!

MY BESTIES

Prologue

Damn, out of all the shit I've done in my life, I never thought that it would end like this. As I look into the eyes of my besties, I see no fear. We came up together, got money together, cried together, killed together, and shit, it looks like we about to lay it down together. We had a great run. We shook this motha fucking city up like dice, for real!

Coming up, all we had was each other. We didn't give a fuck about anybody because nobody gave a fuck about us; feel me? We rode hard in these streets, burning a lot of motha fucka's in the process. What? We E.S.C., East Side Crazy! You better know it! We fucked up, though. We became comfortable when we started sleeping on the enemy and they swarmed our asses like killer bees. As I stand here with my besties ready to meet my maker, I can't help but wonder, *"Did I choose the wrong career path?"* Hearing the hammer cock back on the gun that I'm sure would end our lives; I can't help but to see my life flash before my eyes. The beginning was bad, but this shit right here nigga is death...literally!

*"Money ova everything, self-made
but right now Shawty, you looking
like money, I'm talking real money."*

Ja'ziya 1

"My chick bad looking like a bag of money, I go and get it and she always count it fa me." As I sit here in my room looking out the window bumping to my motivation song, I'm just daydreaming as I always do. I wish I could get a hold of a bag of money. Shit, I'm so broke that I can't even afford a bag of weed.

Damn shame, isn't it? I think I was doomed the second that I came out of my momma's raggedy-ass vagina. My momma was a pretty woman from what I remember. Although, my Aunt Tae told me that she was a rotten bitch on the inside.

She left me with her when I was eight. I'm fifteen now and shit hasn't been right ever since. I think my aunt resents me because she fake-stopped her life to raise me. Shit, she was no better; ghetto ass bitch!

That hoe thinks that she's still in her twenties, walking around here with her pink and blonde hair. Really? She doesn't do shit but sit around the house waiting for her state's check that she gets for her daughter Tyesha and I.

Tyesha is two years younger than I am, but Lil Mama is off the chain. I'm still a virgin, but she's not. She's out there bad and my aunt allows it. She doesn't let me come in the house late or have a nigga call the house without flipping the fuck out on me. My aunt belittles me because I'm by far the prettiest bitch in the house.

My name is Ja`ziya Campbell, but y'all can call me JuJu. I'm 5'6", 155 pounds, and thick in all the right places. I have slanted brown eyes that give me an exotic look. Our ethnic background is Jamaican and Native. I know y'all like that combination.

Yeah, I'm a true rude gal, as I'll whoop a bitch's ass and take names later. Sometimes I don't even take names, fuck them!

I'm not all bad though, I do have goals. I damn sure don't want to be another statistic in the hood, such as a teenage mother or high school dropout. If I could stop fighting, I'd be all right.

Hoes hate on me all the time, which lets me know that I'm doing shit right. No one can hate on a bum bitch, am I right? I'm glad that out of all the bullshit that I've endured throughout my young age; not knowing my father, not having my mother, growing up in an unstable household, and having fucked up people to look up to, I can justly say that I'm not that bad.

I have three people in this world that I can honestly say love me. We literally met in the sandbox. God knew that we were all made for each other, and have been in the same class together since preschool.

First, there's Tamiko, AKA Tiki. We call her "Ms. Smart Mouth" because the shit she says out of anger will make a weaker bitch commit suicide. Standing 4'11", 130 pounds, dark brown eyes that give her a mysterious look, she rocks her hair like Halle Berry. She has an ass so big that you can sit a drink on it and she wouldn't even know it's there. To put icing on the cake, this hoe is bowlegged. She has that "Come Fuck Me" walk down packed. She's the oldest out of the four of us.

All of our birthdays are in the first week of August. With four Leo's on the prowl, trust me; we make shit move when we slide through. Tiki's is first and mine is the third.

Next, there's Elizabeth, AKA Dirty- E, who's birthday is on the fifth of August. We call her "Ms. Know It All" because this bitch knows everything. She knows everybody's business, and can tell you who is fucking who, who's selling what, who robbed who, and when the jump-out boys are coming. How the fuck does she know that shit with her nosey ass? She is my right hand man. She is 5'2", and she weighs 135 pounds. She is high yellow with freckles all over her face. Her large hazel eyes that make her look innocent, but don't sleep on this hoe. She got the name 'Dirty E for a reason. She is the tomboy of the bunch. Well, let me keep it one hundred. This motha fucker is gay as hell. She's the enforcer. Her little ass has been through hell and back growing up, so the term, "Click the Fuck Out" fits right up her alley. I truly think that if we were in a fucked up situation, she'd be the one to come out blazing. Remember that I said that.

Last but not least, we have "Ms. Church Mouse." Randy, AKA ReRe, is the youngest of the crew. Her birthday is August seventh. She fucks with nobody but us. If she doesn't know you, she won't say shit to you. When she was about six years old, her father did some fucked up shit to her body.

When I say that she developed fast, it was an understatement. At fifteen, she is 5'4, weighs 150 pounds, and her chest is a size a 36DD. This little girl measures at 34-24-40. You'd need to see this girl to believe it. This is my baby. She has the prettiest caramel complexion and her eyes are emerald green, courtesy of her white father. Her mother is Latino, so she has this thick, black hair that flows down the middle of her back; beautiful.

But, you know what they say about the quiet ones. We had a run in with some dudes a few weeks ago.

We all attend South Shore High School on 76th and Constance. It's the end of the school year, just before the summer break, so instead of taking the bus, we like to walk down 79th. I stay on 88th and Marquette. It's a nice walk, but we didn't care because 79th be juking.

So on this particular day, we decided to cut up Jeffery and stop at the gas station on 76th. We were all walking, laughing, and having a good time when this light blue Charger with twenty-four inch ice medals was at the light, beating my shit, "Clappers" by Wale.

♫ Shawty got a big ol butt, O YEAHHH! ♫

"That's yo shit, JuJu!"

"E, you know that's my shit!"

Right there on the corner of 76 and Jeffery, I hit that shit. I dropped to the ground on my tippy toes and popped my ass all the way back up. Your girl's a fool with those dance moves. My besties, all except for E of course, started doing the same shit. That's how we move.

The passenger yelled out the window, "A, shawty in the red! What up?" I looked at ReRe and smiled, "Go ReRe, he at you," I teased.

"No Ju, I'm cool. You go."

Knowing that my bestie wasn't feeling him, I politely yelled that she was cool.

We quitted clowning and began walking up the street to our destination, but you couldn't tell some niggas shit! The Charger zoomed to the curb and the dude in the passenger seat hopped out and walked towards us.

"Man, shawty in the red, come here."

This time it was E that said she was cool. Maybe he felt some type of way because E looked just like a nigga.

His old, disrespectful ass had the nerve to say, "Bitch ass nigga, I ain't talking to you." Why'd he say that? We were ready to put our hands and feet on this nigga.

The driver must have sensed that his boy was about to be fucked up because he slowly stepped out of the car. Once his foot hit the pavement, my breath got caught up in my throat. This man had God's hands on him. He had to be at least six' two", with a complexion that was so smooth and chocolaty. His dreads were neat and his razor lining was fresh. He kept it simple in an all-white, Gucci linen short set with pair of Gucci high-tops to match.

Too bad that he was going to get his fine ass fucked up too if he wanted to play, *Captain-Save-A-Nigga*!

"So you wanna be a disrespectful ass nigga?" I said, all up in his face. Out of nowhere, ReRe's crazy ass snatched me back and pushed him against the Charger with her blade to his neck. I mean damn, fuck the small talk, right?

"Hey Shawty, hold up a minute!" His voice was even better than I expected. He walked up to ReRe and calmly placed his hand on her arm, while saying in the most sexist voice ever, "Lil Mama, my boy can be a fool at times. He didn't mean no harm talking the way he was talking. I mean, can you blame him; you tight!"

"Fuck that! This motha fucker needs to know when to show some respect!"

"True, but let me handle my homie."

The dude from the passenger seat stood there with a smug-ass look on his face. He wasn't struggling or anything. The sick bastard looked as if he was enjoying the shit, for real.

ReRe looked at me and I mouthed, "Put it down."

She turned back, looking square in his eyes and the next thing you know, she whipped her hand back so fast that it caused everybody jumped. It happened so fast that I don't even think dude realized that she had nicked him until the blood began trickling down his neck.

"BITCH! YOU CUT ME!"

ReRe gave him the coldest stare that I have ever seen. "You lucky I didn't slice you the fuck up; you disrespectful son of a bitch!"

The driver was now in the middle of us. He wore a nice chain with a pendant hanging from it that read 'LJ'.

"Shawty, what's your name?"

I looked at him and smiled, "JuJu."

"Well Ms. JuJu, like I said before, I apologize for any problems my boy caused today. Let me make it up to you," LJ said.

I looked at him as if he had just spit in my face. "Nigga, you got me fucked up! Your boy wanna be an asshole and now you trying to fuck with me; Nigga beat it!"

I've been through a lot of shit in my past and it has made me tough, so of course I think that I'm *that* bitch. The look this nigga gave me was enough to make me go as mute as a deaf child.

He walked up so close to my face that I could smell the peppermint on his breath. "I'mma let you have that because I know my boy fucked up, but don't get shit twisted. I'm a grown ass man and I do not tolerate disrespect from nobody! Watch yo fucking mouth before I break yo neck!"

On the inside, that turned me the fuck on, but I knew better than to come back with some slick shit. I stepped back and said, "You got that, but don't sleep on us."

I grabbed ReRe and we walked off. LJ looked at me and said, "I'mma see you again, Ms. JuJu and hopefully it will be on better terms."

The dude from the passenger seat got in the car mugging. When he got in the car, he yelled back, "I'mma see yo little ass again."

ReRe shot back, "Not if I don't see you first!"

I didn't know that my girl carried a blade with her. We always had each other's backs no matter what.

School was almost out and we were about to do it big this summer. The only thing was that we were all broke. We were not your average girls from the hood. We were all from the Eastside of Chicago;

from state to the lake, baby! Anyway, we did little schemes here and there to get a little change.

We were not trying to fuck the doughboys in our hood. E wasn't fucking with niggas, period! We had no time to be falling all in love, getting pregnant, or going back and forth from jail with them fools. We surely didn't have time to be falling out at anyone's funerals. Something had to give.

We were some about-it-assed females. We call ourselves Eastside Crazy, (ESC). Our only hope is to get up out of the hood alive, accomplished, and rich. I want to be a nurse. Dirty wants to be a realtor. ReRe wants be a youth counselor, and Tiki wants open her own hair salon. That hoe is a beast with all that hair shit.

We work hard all school year so that we can relax and enjoy our summer breaks. Little did we know that this summer would be one that we would never forget!

"Rolling down the street on some shinning 24's pulling up with chocolate fees and redbones."

Lockjaw 2

"**H**ello!"

"Who is this?"

"You called my phone! Fuck you asking me questions for?"

"Jaw, this your auntie. I'm on 79th and Cottage."

"Good! Hit the liquor store and bring me something to drink."

"I got you. Give me a few minutes."

I hopped out my car and quickly hit the store. There's no standing around this motha fucker! 79th is hot as fish grease! The police are on some good bullshit. Plus, it's the beginning of the summer so I have to stay on my toes around this bitch.

My name is LJ, short for Lockjaw. I got that name when I was a shorty. My mom Dukes said that I used to suck on dirty socks. Fuck y'all! Don't judge me! Anyway, I'm a smooth kind of dude. You could say that I'm somewhat of a ladies man. I'm 6'2" and I weigh 195 pounds. My skin is smooth as chocolate. I rock dreads, but I keep them tight. I'm young and I'm getting it to say the least. I just turned nineteen on May second and I'm already sitting on a lovely nest egg that's worth of over six figures.

I started selling drugs at a young age out in the projects where I was born and raised. Back in the day, the Robert Taylor high-rise buildings were a gold mine. I saw my Uncle DB and my father getting it when I was younger. They would never let me in on the action, so when I was old enough to make moves, I started as a lookout and I quickly worked my way up the ranks.

At the age of fifteen, I began moving weight. The scariest moment I had selling drugs happened when I was running my own trap spot. I had just copped my last brick and I was bagging it up when my phone rang.

"Yo Jaw, my man's wanna come holla at you."

"Who the fuck is ya man's?"

"Calm down dude, he cool."

"He better be, cause if he try any dumb shit, I'mma light his ass up like the firework show at Navy Pier on the 4th of July."

"Fair enough."

I get up and check my38 revolver snub nose. What? Yeah, I got a 38. It'll server its purpose.

KNOCK! KNOCK!

"Who is it?"

"Poohman sent me."

I opened the door and my heart dropped to my damn socks.

"Damn Uncle! I didn't know you was coming-."

That's all I got out before my Uncle DB put his paws on a nigga. That was the worst ass whooping I ever received in my life. I tried my hardest to get his big ass up off of me.

"Lockjaw, your father would kill me if he knew I bought shit from you!"

"Man, I'm doing me. I'm trying to take care of my mom Dukes and my siblings. I'm doing what he ain't doing."

"Nephew, this life ain't for you. Wait a minute; I'm coming up here to get some work, and I'm getting it from you? How long have you been serving?"

"Man Uncle, I been serving since I was like nine."

"Ain't that bout a bitch!"

"Uncle, I been grown for a while and this is what it is. No disrespect to you, but I'mma keep doing me."

He never told my father what I was doing. He did however upgrade my little 38. He gave me my first big gun. It was a Desert Eagle and was my favorite gun. Other than Poohman, I really didn't socialize with niggas.

I really didn't even have a girl. The buildings talk. These little hoes knew who was getting dough.

I wasn't trying to let one of these hood boogers trap me, no sir!

When I was seventeen, I thought I was in love. I ended up having two kids by my girl at the time. I love my kids to death, but their mama can't be trusted. These hoes aren't loyal.

Needless to say, I take good care of my babies, but their mama can eat a dick! I'm just saying. It's now two years later and I'm doing better than most.

I don't trick because I got it. A bitch better have their own. I don't mind treating, but you must show me that you are worth it. I got a few bust downs that I entertain when I want my dick wet. I do want a wife one day. That's another reason why I'm not too flashy.

I got a little Charger with some bang and some 24's, nothing fancy. I want my chick to be smart and well educated. I can't stand a stupid bitch. I'd kiss the moon if I could find a virgin, but finding a virgin would be harder than finding that bitch Carmen San Diego. I'm just saying.

I like them 5'5 or 5'6 and thick in all the right places. I like them with a caramel complexion and sexy as fuck, but not too thick. Some of that shit doesn't look right when you take their clothes off. I would prefer you have your own hair, but now days you never know. As long as you keep that shit done, I'm good.

I like them feisty, but not disrespectful. Let's be clear, I don't play that ignorant shit. I'll shake the fuck out a bitch. I might even slap fire from their ass, depending on what they did. Hold up, my phone ringing.

"Yo!"

"Damn, where the fuck you at?"

"My bad Auntie Boo, I'm on my way now."

On my way to my auntie's. I called Poohman and told him to get ready.

"I'm outside, my dude."

Poohman came out of the crib looking like a hot ass mess. This nigga is crazy! My man's got on a black long sleeve t-shirt with some black and green army fatigue shorts and he had the nerve to wear wheat-colored Timbs.

Really my nigga? Ok, we do live in the Windy City, but we got hot ass summers too. I know my dude's feet are hot as shit. Then this fool still got that bandage around his neck from when that little shawty barely cut his ass.

I'm not even going to front; shawty had the look of death in her eyes when she upped that blade on my homie. Quiet as kept, my boy liked that shit. He likes them old crazy ass broads that stab him and shit.

I'mma break a bitch's face if they up a blade on me. That shit has been on my mind for a minute. I can't get Ms. JuJu off of my mind. She was fucking beautiful. I loved her feistiness. That smart-ass mouth and those eyes. Damn! Shawty was like that. That little bitch's mouth is her only shortcoming. I couldn't allow her to talk to me like that no matter how cute she is. I'm a man!

(SLAM)

"Nigga, don't slam my fucking door like that, pussy!"

"Fuck yo soft ass up in here daydreaming about with that sexy ass smile on your face?"

I looked at my homie, "Fuck you and them hot ass boots you got on!"

*****

When we pulled up to my Auntie Boo's block and people were everywhere. Niggas were all over the corners, the fire hydrant was on at the other end of the street, and you could smell the barbeque in the air. "Damn, I hope Boo grilling because I'm hungry as shit," Poohman said.

"Nigga you always hungry."

I pulled over in front of my auntie's crib and I saw her high yellow-ass sitting on the porch with a card table gambling.

"Yo thirsty ass going take the bid anyway." I hear my auntie talking to her pinochle partner as I walk up to the porch.

"What up auntie?" She looked at Lil Mama and said, "Oh, hold up hoe; let me get my beer"Lil Mama laughed. "Yo thirsty ass."

"Hoe don't hate," my auntie said.

Lil Mama is my auntie's best friend. They met while doing a FED bid. Yeah, I said FED bid. My auntie was out here doing her mafucking mutha fucking thing and these hoe-ass niggas out here were mad, so they put the alphabet boys in her life.

Now Lil Mama is straight gangsta. This bitch pulled some Set-It-Off-type shit. Her and some goofy ass nigga robbed a bank. Now that's my type of bitch! They got away, but her ass got caught for doing some other shit. That's some hoe ass shit, but doing eight years did her some justice.

She's fine as fuck. I've got a nasty ass crush on her. She's 5'6, weighs about 160 pounds, and has curly black hair. Her hair is natural and sexy. She has these eyes that make me want to stare into them all day. That's some lame ass shit, right? Fuck y'all! She bad!

"Damn, why you staring, Jaw? See something you like?" Lil Mama asked while looking at me with those *fuck-me* eyes. I swear I saw those eyes before.

"Bitch stop flirting with my nephew and melt."

As always, my auntie was hating so I moved back to the front yard and went to holla at some niggas that I knew.

"You want beef? I got that.
Dope? I got that. Hoes? I got that.
Dro? I got that. Money? I got that.
Cars? I got that. Pistols? I got that.
Niggas get shot at."

Dirty & 3

"Elizabeth, come downstairs and take this trash out."

"Why I gotta do it?"

"Because Jae`lyn is at work and since you think you a boy, it won't kill your ass."

Sometimes I want to punch my mom in her shit. She always has something smart to say about my sexual preference. I didn't have to come out of the closet, but I came out of her pussy gay, no bullshit!

I used to always get my ass beat because no matter what, I wasn't wearing a motherfucking dress. I'm the second child born to Haitian immigrants. My mom was eight months pregnant when they moved to Chicago. My dad was very supportive. When she went into labor, he was there, breathing with her, throughout the whole nine yards.

The second that I came out of my mom's pussy, this ol' disrespectful motha fucker actually stole my mom in the face and walked out of the room screaming, "That's the devils child; not mine." I was white as hell. Both of my parents are blue black.

My mom swore that she never stepped out on him. He stayed, but he treated me like shit. He would beat me, starve me, and make me do some fucked-up shit to him. I don't want to elaborate, but I want y'all to get to know me and know why I turned out the way that I did.

He drank and smoked weed that was laced with cocaine. My mom worked two jobs to support us so she was gone a lot. On the days that she would work, he would make me watch him masturbate.

Then he would ejaculate in my face. Unfortunately, that was a good day.

On a bad day, he would make me suck his dick until my jaws were sore. He started fucking with me when I was about four. It ended about five years later when I ended his life.

I told my mom what he was doing. She would just tell me to pray about it and eventually he would stop, but I guess God didn't fuck with me like that. I didn't need God for what I planned to do.

It was my ninth birthday and my mom had planned a small party with just my besties and me. She rented a bunch of movies and bought us a gang of junk food. We ate, had a good time, and fell asleep.

Later that night, I woke up to use the restroom and I saw that ReRe wasn't next to me anymore. I went room to room looking for her. I approached my parent's room and I could hear small cries. I heard my father saying, "Shut the fuck up bitch." I knew it was ReRe. My heart broke into pieces because I couldn't help her. I went back to the living room crying. I just wanted him to be quick. I needed her to come back and go to sleep because I was getting his ass tonight.

Ten minutes later, she laid next to me crying, "He hurt me E!" I told her to go back to sleep. I knew she had fallen asleep because her grip on my arm loosened. I knew it was now or never.

I walked back to my parent's room and could hear my father snoring loudly. I got on my knees and crawled under the bed to where I knew my father kept his lock box. I opened the box as quietly as I could and felt around for a few seconds until I found what I was looking for.

When I used to cry and refuse to pleasure him, he would point this gun at me. He even stuck it down there before. I stood up and walked to the side of the bed. I turned the gun sideways to click the safety button off, and when I looked up, my father was staring at me.

The last thing he said before I blew his brains out was, "You are the child of the devil."

Back to the present, my mom resents me. His murder was labeled a robbery gone wrong. Deep down inside, she knew what I did. Oh fucking well. Shit, she could get it too. I love my mom, but she could have done more to stop the nigga. Fuck it! Let me call my bestie, JuJu and see what time we are going to her Godmother's barbeque.

"I'm sucka duckie, I'm sucka free,
you ain't a G, don't fuck with me,
I'm suckin niggas outta style, G season.
I'm suckin niggas outta style, G season."

ℑiki 4

Bout time y'all motha fuckers got to my chapter. My name is Tamiko, AKA Tiki. As you may already know me, Ju, ReRe, and Dirty E are like sisters and brothers. We are all Leo's and we get along so good. It's all real. None of that phony shit that y'all are used to see. Them my motha fuckers! We E.S.C. until the death of us. If you ask me, we all get along so good because we all have horrible past's that fucked us all up.

My own mama can't stand me because I look just like my father. She was his side bitch back in the day when he was on the come up. She was just like all the other hood rats in the hood. She thought that if she got pregnant then she would lock my father down. Wrong! He told her he wasn't ready for kids. He gave her four hundred dollars to get an abortion.

This trifling ass hoe went to the mall and bought a few outfits. Needless to say, when he found out what she did, he found her and tried to abort me himself. From what my aunt told me, he beat her within an inch of her life. On the way to the hospital, she flat lined twice. She pulled through and I came three months early. I was four pounds even. Other than me being a premature baby, I was good.

My mom's fake ass didn't raise me. She was too busy chasing baller dick. My Aunt Rose raised me until I was seven. She died after overdosing from too much heroine. I guess my mom had somewhat of a heart because she took me in. Although, I think that I would have been better off in foster care.

She had a slew of niggas in and out of our tiny ass two-bedroom apartment. A few of them even tried to make their way into my bed. I got tired of that shit. I started running away to E's crib.

When I was about ten, I was walking back from Bessmer Park when this black two-door Infiniti Coupe rolled up on me. My scared ass was about to run. Shit, motha fuckers still be kidnapping kids. I'll be damned if I end up in somebody's basement as a sex slave. Bullshit!

He rolled the window down and said, "Tamiko."

I said, "Who the fuck is you?"

He chuckled and said, "Yeah, you definitely my baby. Come here."

Curiosity got the best of me because I walked over to his car. "I'm yo Daddy! Get in!"

I looked at him as if he was crazy. "What's my mama name?

"Sharon."

That was all I needed to hear. I hopped in and he asked me where we stayed. When we walked into the apartment, we found my mom's trifling ass on all fours getting fucked by a man I called Uncle Larry.

When she saw whom I was with, the look on her face let me know that the words he spoke were biblical. She jumped up so fast that you would have thought she was in a martial arts movie.

"Oh my Lord, Meechie what you doing here?"

He stared at my mom with a stare that would have made the Grim Reaper kill himself. I guess my mama felt it too, because she pissed all over herself right there in the middle of the living room.

"Tiki come on, you don't live here no more." Shit, Daddy or not, I got to get up outta this hellhole. BYE FELICIA! Life after that was heaven. He kept me in the same school after I told him about my besties. He told me how he met my mama. Shit, he even told me about the time he almost killed us. I didn't think my life was worth shit anyway, because of whose vagina I came out of. I wasn't even mad.

He told me I had a brother that was two years younger than I was. I was just happy to finally be happy. On my eleventh birthday, I woke up mad because I had to go to school. I got happy when my

Daddy told me he was taking my besties and me to Great America and the mall in Gurnee Mills. I couldn't sit still in class. Shit, neither could my besties. We were all so happy.

Finally, at 2:30, it was time to go. My Daddy's car wasn't across the street in his normal parking spot. No big deal. Sometimes I have to catch the bus home. I told my friends to go home and get ready as soon as I changed we was coming to scoop them.

I never made it to the bus stop. "Birthday girl, want a ride?"

"Daddy, you late."

"I know, boo. I had some errands to run."

On the way home, I wanted my usual sugar fix. See, every day we stop at the gas station on 76 and Stony Island. I always get some tropical skittles and a red chilly willy.

When we pulled into the gas station, my Daddy seemed like he was nervous about something. He handed me a hundred dollar bill. "Daddy gotta make a phone call."

When I saw that hundred-dollar bill, I jumped out of that car so fast that you would have thought it was on fire. I walked in the store as if I had a million dollars. You couldn't tell me shit. I was about to buy everything in there. When I got to the counter, I rang up $55.45 worth of junk food. Hey, it's my birthday. He won't be mad, right?

Walking back to my Daddy's car, I could hear him yelling at somebody on the phone. "Fuck you nigga! Do you know who I am? I will bury yo ass, pussy!"

As I closed the door, he hung up the phone. "Did my baby buy the whole store?" His smile was a mirror of mine and I loved to see him smile. Sadly, that would be the last time that I saw it.

After we left the gas station, we headed home. It was rush hour and traffic was crazy. We took Stoney Island north. We ended up on 67th. Sitting at the light we were rocking to Twista's "Pimp Like Me." My Daddy loved this song. We were so busy rocking our heads and singing that he didn't see the man approaching our car.

Before I could scream, he blew my Daddy's brains all over my face and clothes. The last memory I have of my Daddy was he dying on my birthday. I hate thinking about that shit. It puts a damper on my mood.

Even though I only had him around for one year that was the best year of my life. My mom all but laughed in my face when I had to come back home. She never changed for me. I still live with her now. She didn't have to change for me. The full-blown AIDS that she has made her seem different.

We barely talk. But fuck all that shit! I'm alive, sexy as shit, and ready to live my life. Like my girl JuJu, I'm still a virgin. I'm not trying to have babies or catch the kill-kill. We still say ReRe's a virgin because the shit that her sick ass father did to her doesn't count.

Aww shit! Talking to y'all, I'mma be late for JuJu's auntie barbeque. Let me call this girl before I have to curse her ass out.

ReRe 5

S ometimes I hate being alone. The demons from my past keep my mind consumed with anger and rage. I could never bring a child into the world because the person that helped bring me into the world decided that instead of loving and guiding me in the right path, he'd rather use my body and me for his own sick and perverted pleasures. My mother was also fucked up in the head because she used to help him. All I know is pain, shame, and loneliness. I remember when my Daddy first hurt me.

I used to always hear my parents arguing about the smallest things. One argument I heard changed everything. "Papi, you can't! She's your daughter!"

"You can do this small simple thing or I'm leaving! Then who's gonna take care of you and that little bitch?"

"I won't do it!"

The talking stopped so I got up from the couch to eavesdrop. That's when I saw my father fucking my mother in the ass as if she was less than human. That's not even the worst part. She was in a deep heroine nod. To control her, he would keep her high.

I thought I could ease back to the couch without being seen, but as I did, I looked up and saw my father looking at me while he pounded my mother's ass as if he was digging for gold. The next few days were the worst. Before it all became a blur, I remember my mother being extra nice to me.

"Mami, let's play dress up. You can put on Mommy's pink dress."

"Ohhh, and Mommy can I wear your makeup?"

I remember looking up and seeing tears fall from her eyes.

"Yes, you can. Let Mommy make you look pretty."

I remember looking in the mirror at my face, clothes, and hair. I swear I felt like a princess.

"You look good, baby. Now come sit next to Mommy and let me make you feel good."

"Ouch Mommy! That hurt! Why you hitting my arm like that?"

"This will just hurt for a few minutes."

She pulled out a needle filled with white stuff and stuck me in the arm.

"OUCH MOMMY! Tha…Tha…That feels good. Mommy, what's that?"

I looked up to see my father coming in the room butt-ass naked. "Look at Daddy's baby. Let Daddy make you feel good."

The sexual abuse went on like that for three years. I was eight when I finally had the nerve to speak up. Not only did the sexual abuse continue, but the drug abuse did as well. I finally told my teacher that my father was molesting me and shooting heroine into my veins.

She was floored! CPS got involved and I was eventually taken from my parents. I went to a foster home that allowed my father to have unsupervised visits with me. Talk about the system failing you! The abuse didn't stop until my father was sent to prison for murdering my mother.

I was numb to a lot of shit. I didn't have a normal childhood. I liked school because I had three friends who loved me for me. I love them with all my heart and I would kill for them. Hell, they had their own problems too. Even E's father messed with me. Shit was crazy. I'll never forget that night that she killed him.

After he hurt me, E held me until I fell asleep. Playing possum is what I did best. I let her think I was asleep. She left and went back to her parent's room. I waited for a good thirty seconds and then I followed her.

I heard him say, "You are the child of the devil," and then, POW! I didn't even run. I walked

up to her and told her to come back to t
room and lay down as if nothing happened.

She wiped the gun off and threw it
dumpster behind the house. We left the bac
open and went to lay back next to JuJu and
who by this time were wide-awake also.

"Did you kill him?" JuJu asked.

"Yeah, Ju, I did."

"Fuck him!"

We laid awake pretending to be asleep until w
could no longer ignore the screams roaring from the
depths of E's mother's soul.

"LAWD A MERCY! WHYYYYY? HE DEAD!
HELP ME LAWD, PLEASE!"

She knew he was a rotten motha fucker, but
damn did she love his sick ass. We never uttered a
word to no one. We got each other's back. They
helped me with my nightmares. Mostly every night,
I relive my childhood. My father still tries to reach
out to me. The nerve!

I moved in with my father's sister. She's all
right, but she doesn't give a fuck what I do. My

besties are all I need. Speaking of my besties let me call and see what's cracking with this barbeque. DUECES!

"Who run the world; girls!
Who run the world; girls!
Who run this mother? Girls!"

JuJu 6

It's time to get flyer than that thing. Today's my friend's auntie's barbeque. The block is going to be packed. Food's going to be good and niggas gonna be flocking. I'm geeked just thinking about it. Everybody and their mammie is going to be out there so you know my besties and I are going to show up and show out. It's mandatory!

Today, I'mma live up to my nickname, Ms. *I'm That Bitch*, because when I make my way through, I demand attention. Why? Because, I'M THAT BITCH!

Today I'm rocking my sheer dark grey maxi dress. It's sexy, but classy. I'll keep it simple with my hair. A bun at the top of my head should do. It's hot, plus I want the attention on my blemish-free face. My light brown slanted eyes do damage if you look into them.

"Where my girls at? Damn, my phone ringing."

I felt around my bed and grabbed it before it stops.

"Hey skank! We at the door."

"Come up then."

"Yo ghetto ass auntie on that bullshit."

I hung up in Tiki's face and stomped down the stairs with a full-blown attitude.

"Lil girl, you better stop stomping down my stairs before I stomp yo ass! And where you think you going in that tight ass dress?"

I let my friends in and I turn around to answer her question. "I'm going to Boo's barbeque."

"Did you ask me?"

"No, I didn't think I had to since Lil Mama gon be there."

"I don't give a fuck about no damn Lil Mama! Fuck her! I raised you! I feed and clothe you! That bitch thinks she's all that! That's why she did eight years in prison! Stupid ass bank robbing bitch!"

I couldn't believe this ol' ungrateful-ass hoe. My Auntie Lil Mama did hit a few banks awhile back. She got caught because my Auntie Tae was out there stunting as if she was the one getting money.

She got drunk one night and said too much around the wrong motha fucker. That person turned my auntie in for the reward money. She left my greedy ass Auntie Tae everything! House, car, and some money. Tae did her wrong. She barely sent her anything. She did her time like a G though. When she came home, she felt back as if it was nothing. I know my auntie. She was just waiting on the right time. When she's ready, she's going to fuck Tae's ass up.

To be honest with you, I don't think she gave Tae everything. She's too relaxed about the situation. Then again, after eight years, wouldn't you be a little calmer too?

"How you gon talk about her like that when this is her house? That truck you driving, hers too."

"Who you talking to like that? Don't get embarrassed!"

I guess E had enough. My auntie always had a soft spot for her anyway. "Damn Tae, chill. You looking sexy as usual today."

I rolled my eyes. This ol' thirsty-ass hoe had the nerve to smile. "Thank you baby. Tell Irene to call me." She rolled her eyes at me and walked off.

"She wanna fuck you E."

"Fuck you Ju!"

I stepped back to admire my besties outfits. Okay I was impressed. ReRe had on this Baby Phat cotton romper. Her hips and ass were on full display. "Damn ReRe, you trying to catch you one, huh?"

With us she's so silly. She walked in the middle of our little circle and made her ass thunderclap saying, "Shawty gotta big ol butt, ohh yeah."

We all fell out laughing. E was in this hoe looking mighty sexy with her Chicago Bulls jersey on. The back had my number one player on it. D Rose, of course! She killed it with the all-white Roca Wear shorts and buried the game with some red, black, and white Jordans. Her waves were making me seasick!

"Damn E, what bitch you trying to make chase you today?"

"Ju don't be J. I'm on one shawty."

"Whatever!"

Tiki looked like a true diva. My bestie had on this all-white cotton maxi dress like mine except her whole back was out. She had on some cute beige wedges.

"Tiki over here looking like a glass of whole milk and shit."

She smiled at me on the way out the door and said, "Well you know milk does a body good! Let's roll!"

We stepped out of my door looking like a thousand bucks. We weren't anywhere near millionaire status, but you sure couldn't tell us shit! The barbeque must have been juking because we heard the music all the way down here. We walked from 88th and Marquette. As we crossed 87th street, I heard all the 'ooh's' and 'ahh's' from the block boys.

This one little cutie named Woodie said, "Damn Juju, you make me wanna leave home!"

I shot back, "You can't hug the block and this coochie at the same time."

"I ain't going nowhere. I'mma get you girl."

"Boy bye!"

LJ

"Man Auntie Boo, this little block party is cracking. It's some cute little broads out here." My auntie's friend Lil Mama looked at me and smiled, "You ain't seen cute yet. Wait until my niece and her little crew get here and shuts this motha fucker down."

I looked at Lil Mama' sexy ass and said, "Since I know I'm too young for you, please tell me that your niece is as fine as you."

Lil Mama chuckled and had the nerve to blush, boosting a nigga's ego. "Today is your lucky day because she looks just like me. Speaking of the devil, here they come walking up the street now."

I stood up and looked in the direction that she was pointing. Before I could say anything, Poohman's hotheaded ass jumped up off the porch and said, "There go that little hoe that cut me."

JuJu

"JuJu, if you switch any harder, you gon break yo hips."

"Don't hate! Don't hate bitch! Learn to appreciate!"

We too damn goofy. I love my besties. As we crossed the street, I looked up and I almost fainted. "Re, ain't this a bitch? Tell me that ain't the ol' boy you cut standing up in Boo's yard!"

ReRe's hand shot to her purse. "Hell yeah, that's him. Let him turn up and I'mma turn his ass down real quick!"

LJ

"Damn auntie that's shawty and her little crew that I told you about." Boo stood up. "I'll be damned. I shoulda known. Ja`ziya bring yo ass here right now."

JuJu

"Damn y'all, Boo's ol' ignorant ass just called my government like that." There was few people in the yard when we walked up. Shit, my besties and I were ready for whatever! I got ready to hit the stairs when the passenger dude jumped in my way. I looked at him and smiled. I had to be on my best behavior since my auntie Lil Mama was watching.

"Excuse me; I'm trying to get past."

This clown was unaware of what hood he was in, said, "Bitch you got a pass, you won't get another one."

WHAAAATTTT? Before I could say anything, my auntie came walking down the stairs. "Poohman, out of respect for Jaw, I'mma let you get that pass, but if you call her another bitch, I'mma show you what eight years of frustration look like." She paused for a minute to let that threat sink in. "Do I make myself clear, baby?"

He looked at Jaw for some help. Shit, that nigga put his head down.

"I got you, little Mama."

I walked up the stairs and sat in the seat that my auntie was in. LJ watched me the whole time, but didn't say a word. He had this, "Hell Naw" look on his face. Boo watched the whole exchange. "Damn Jaw, close your mouth, or speak."

Jaw

This is a small world, I swear. I've been thinking about
this chick for a minute. Come to find out, she's my auntie's Goddaughter. Crazy! I look at my man's and this nigga's mugging the fuck out of the ol' girl that cut his ass. Shit, she mugging his ass right back like, "Nigga what."

"Poohman let me holla at you." I see it all in my boy's eyes. He want's to say something. As soon as we hit the kitchen, I go in. "What up, Poohman? Let that shit go, my nigga."

He shook his head and what he said next confirmed what I always thought. This nigga is crazy. "A, you think shawty gon give me her number?"

ReRe

I see the way this nigga's mugging. I swear he's not about that life! I came prepared for anybody's dumb shit. I already planned it out. I'mma mace the crowd first, and then I'mma start slicing motha fuckers. What? I don't play games when it comes to my besties safety and me. I look at JuJu on the porch talking to her auntie and Boo and we lock eyes.

I feel like we can communicate with our eyes. It's as if I heard her say in my mind, "You okay?" I winked my eye and shook my head yes. She smiled and continued her conversation. My stomach started growling, reminding me that I haven't eaten all day.

"Auntie Lil Mama, where's all the cooked food at?"

"It's in the house, baby. Help yourself."

She didn't have to tell me twice. E and Tiki's greedy asses already had their food. Their asses were sitting in some lawn chairs in the yard fucking up some ribs. "Y'all bogus! Where my plate at?"

E's silly ass said, "We kept calling you when we hit the yard, but yo crazy was in cut a nigga mode so we left yo ass standing there."

"Fuck y'all!"

Tiki looked up from her food and said, "No thank you, but I know somebody who looks like they wouldn't mind rubbing ya fluffy."

"Smart mouth hoe!"

"Girl, go eat!"

I walked in the house with one thing on my mind, food! As I approached the kitchen, I heard voices. "Why you tripping? Let that shit go, my nigga!"

I instantly pulled my blade out thinking that this nigga wants to act a fool. I'll cut his ass up for real this time. Who the fuck does he think this is? I'm no punk. I'm about to come around the corner swinging. Just before I made my move, I hear the passenger dude say, "A, you think shawty gon give me her number?"

That shit almost made me bust up laughing. This motha fucker's crazy. Quiet as kept, that shit made my little kitty twitch. I haven't had the desire to become sexually active on my own, but this nigga's style had me tweaking. Lost in my own thoughts, I didn't even realize that they stopped talking and when I looked up, they were standing in front of me.

"Damn, you gon cut us both, little killa?" The nigga known as Poohman licked his lips and put his hands in his pockets. Seeing that he wasn't on no bullshit, I put my blade back in my purse. I looked at him and smiled.

"So you want my number; huh?"

JuJu

I'm having a good time chilling with my besties and my old heads. I swear I want to be just like them. They're some G's for real. Boo a beast! Sitting here listening to her stories, I'm glad that I'm not on her bad side. Now my auntie Lil Mama's been a beast. I used to love when she would come over to Auntie Tae's house.

Tae hated how close we were. Lil Mama always made sure I had whatever I needed. I wish she would have let me live with her, but I knew she ran those streets. She made sure she saw me every day and she always told me that she loved me. She treated my besties the same way.

"Ju, go get me and Boo another drink."

"Can I get one?"

"You can get this ass whooping!"

"Never mind, then. I'm going auntie."

I got up and went into the house. No sooner than I hit the corner, I see LJ, Poohman, and ReRe standing around looking crazy. "What the fuck?" I went straight into beast mode. "Y'all trying to pull it with my girl on the low? I will tear this motha fucker up! ReRe, you ready?"

I'll be damned if all three of their asses looked at me and started rolling.

"What the fuck I miss?

Re looked at me and said, "I'm cool. Poohman and I got some things to talk about. Jaw, take my bestie and give us a few minutes."

I looked at ReRe as if she had three heads. This hoe doesn't talk to strangers, especially niggas.

"Okay, you sure you cool?"

She smiled and said, "Jaw like you JuJu. Give the boy some play."

And just like that, what started off as a tense situation quickly became a breakthrough moment for my bestie. I'm happy too. Jaw is a cutie! We kicked it hard for the rest of the day. E and Tiki even warmed up to them. I'm glad I got me boo thang. God is good!

Will he answer our prayers when we bite off more than we can chew?

"I be repping my city, I be
repping my city, err, err, err night!"

Big Moe 7

"Everybody get the fuck on the ground, right fucking now! You, fill this bag up and bitch if you wanna go home tonight, don't pass me no dye packs! Try me and I'mma murder yo whole family!"

This hoe snatched the bag and started throwing that money in there so fast you would have thought that she was robbing the bank with me! I've been robbing shit for years. I think I hit my first lick when I was seven. I robbed the candy lady that lived in my building.

My name is Ramon, but everybody calls me Big Moe. I got that name because I've got heart. I went from robbing the candy lady to sticking up doughboys that served out of the building I grew up in. Born and raised in one of the most dangerous housing projects called Cabrini Green, I had to do me to survive.

My mom was murdered when I was a baby. Don't know my punk-ass father. My G-ma raised me. She had seven kids and ten grandkids that she also raised. Food and clothes were limited. My G-ma was gangsta! No matter what I did, she had my back. I robbed a motha fucker; she hid me in the house. When I shot a nigga, she got rid of the evidence. When I got a hoe pregnant, it was she that either took em to the clinic for that abortion or helped me buy clothes, pampers, and other shit.

I got three kids that I claim. Fucking project hoes always want to trap a nigga on the come up. Through it all, my G-ma had me. The whole Cabrini Green loved my G-ma. She could break any nigga on the dice game. She would smoke and drink your ass under the table. I thought she would be with me forever.

We never kept secrets and that's why I loved her so much. She had cancer and she didn't tell us until she was on her deathbed. The love that I had for women died with her.

I've been raining terror on this city ever since. Fuck a nigga, fuck a hoe. I'm trying to get money! I don't fuck with no outside motha fuckers. I keep it all in the family. I roll with two niggas and two niggas only. My cousins JR and Boogie, who're brothers.

Niggas ain't built like us these days. Feel me? After I robbed every nigga in the 312 area code, I began casing banks. Why banks? Because drug dealers aren't holding like that. This little slut I was fucking a while back was a bank teller at a bank around the downtown Chicago area. I liked the hoe. She had the nerve to have her priorities in order. She had no kids, had her own crib, and she drove a beamer. I was impressed, but I would never tell her ass that shit. Fuck for? She was an easy fuck.

Nothing more, nothing less. No love for these hoes, remember?

Anyway, she gave me the whole layout of the bank that she worked at. I put my cousins on the lick. The shit was too sweet to pass up. I wasn't fucking with outside niggas on this, period. I am not to be trusted. Fuck around and rob his hoe ass when we finish the job.

We ended up pulling the job off with no problems. We got almost forty grand. Not bad for two minutes. After that, we were hooked! I ended up murking the little bitch that put me on the robbery. Why? Because I wasn't treating her as she wanted to be treated and I didn't need her having that type of shit on me. Oh well! There's plenty of pussy in Chicago.

It isn't as if I'm an ugly dude. I'm six foot three and 195 pounds. Caramel complexion and the seal dealer is that I've got hazel and green eyes. The hoes can't resist these eyes. Must run in the family because Boogie and JR got them too.

We only choose banks with young and dumb tellers. Wine and dine their asses for a few days and then, BAM! We got the whole layout. We hit the licks with no problems. Then we dispose of the bitches that gave us the info.

Today's lick was all Boogie's. He had this little bitch going in a matter of days. "Man Joe, we got thirty seconds! Let's move out! Everybody stay where the fuck y'all at and don't move!"

As we made our way to the door I heard, "POP!" I already knew it was Boogie finishing the job. Mission accomplished!

After we counted the take, that shit came out to be almost $350,000.00. We did well this time. "JR, take this doe over East. We gon lay low for a few days, my niggas. This shit gon be on the news for a few days."

When we hit licks over east, we had a stash spot over there. If we hit licks west of the Dan Ryan expressway, we hide that shit in my storage building past Cicero.

"I'm bout to go get some pussy."

"Money, money, money, money."

The Come Up 8

Juju

Two weeks after the barbeque, Jaw and I are still kicking it tough. Jaw is cool as shit. He's funny, laid back, and reserved. He has an old soul, but that's okay. Today my boo wants to take me out to eat and shop. We deserve some quality time together since his ass likes to hit the streets.

"I wanna go to Ford City mall, boo."

He looks at me with the sexist grin on his face. "Whatever you want, Ju."

I love when he calls me that. I called ReRe to see if she wanted to double date since her and

Poohman have been together every day since the barbeque as well. "Hello."

"Hey hooker, you and Poohman wanna go to the mall with us?"

I heard her put her hand over the phone. "Yeah, we'll meet y'all. Where you at?"

"At Jaw's crib."

"We on the way."

Dirty E

"A, little man, run in the store and get me a beef taco with a large fry. Make sure they put mild sauce on my fries, and get me a Pepsi."

Shorty ran right past my homie. "What up, Pancho?"

The nigga Pancho is responsible for us getting our dough. He put us on all the drug dealers that think that they're doing something. Quiet as kept, I think he helped us set motha fuckers up because he's too scared to bust his own gun. Pussy-ass motha fucker!

I told JuJu that if he starts acting funny, I'mma kill his ass.

"E Man Joe, I've been trying to get at you."

Just then, little man ran out the store. "E, here you food go."

"Thanks little man. Wait, where's my change little nigga?"

This little bastard can't be any older than eleven. Shorty's little badass had the nerve to tell me, "Nigga I waited in that long ass line. Yo change is my tip."

After he said that, he took off before I could grab his punk ass.

"E, I been trying to get at you. Come hit a few blocks with me."

We got in his Tahoe. This scary ass nigga didn't say shit until we got on the expressway.

"My little sister's been fucking with some nigga from The Greens, and he and his peoples getting dough."

I looked at his ass as if he had just said, *"Fuck my besties."*

"Nigga, we ain't fucking with them projects. You crazy as hell."

"Let me finish. The nigga name JR. He and his family be hitting banks around Chicago."

"And nigga? Get to the point."

"When they hit banks close to the Eastside, they hide the money over on Marquette. They laying low for a few days. Thing is, they gon move the money tomorrow."

When he said that, I got to thinking. "How much?"

"She said it's almost $350,000.00."

I almost choked on my damn taco.

"Nigga, don't spill that in here."

"Nigga, fuck you! I helped you get this bitch!"

He waited a few minutes and then said, "So, y'all gon do it?"

I picked up my phone and called JuJu. "A code four. Meet me at the spot!"

JuJu

I was having a nice time with my dude until a code four ended all that. No matter what it was about, it was time to end the fun. Period! I pulled ReRe aside and put her up on game. LJ and Poohman were in Finish Line copping us the latest Jordan's.

"Bae, we got a family emergency."

My poor boo looked concerned. "What? What happened? You good Ma?"

"Jaw, I'm good. It's just that I need to see what my auntie wants."

I don't want to start off lying to him, but how we dough isn't his business.

"Damn Ju! I'm salty as shit, but it is what it is."

Damn, its' time to do damage control. "Let me just see what's going on. When I finish, I'mma call you so you can come get me; okay?"

"Alright, let's roll."

Dirty E

"Tiki, where you at? When you finish, meet us at the spot."

ReRe, JuJu, and I sat impatiently, waiting for Tiki to finish doing somebody's damn hair.

"So, what did Pancho say?"

I looked at JuJu and said, "You know the rules boo-boo. We all must be here. I'm waiting on Tiki."

She rolled her eyes, huffed, and puffed. That shit don't faze me. She does that shit whenever she doesn't get her way.

We came up with code four in fifth grade. When we say it, it means emergency and when you have an emergency, you do what? Get together to see what's good.

"Here comes Tiki," JuJu and ReRe said at the same damn time.

"Alright, from what Pancho told me, the money's still there. His sister said that this JR dude is supposed to move the money in the morning, so we move tonight."

"TONIGHT?"

I knew I was going to get that reaction. "Yes tonight! What? Y'all scared?" I knew that would get them going.

Ms. *I'm That Bitch* was the first to speak. "You know we ain't scared. It's just, this is a lot of money, and I'm sure this shit ain't gon be that simple."

She had a point. "Look, Pancho said that he's been watching the spot. Dudes got this crib as a safe house. His dumb ass really didn't do his homework on the neighborhood. I know everything that comes and goes through this motha fucker. Come on y'all. We got this!"

I saw the uneasy look that JuJu gave me, so I knew that telling her after the lick I was killing Pancho was out of the question, for now at least! Tiki was the only one not talking.

"Speak your mind, *Ms. Smart Mouth*."

She looked at me and said, "This is some short notice ass shit and it's a suicide mission, but you already know I'm ready for whatever! This our hood! Let's get this money!"

I looked at JuJu and said, "We need you boo. We gon be alright."

JuJu stood up and finally said, "What time we doing this?"

"At sunset. That's about two hours from now so let's get ready!"

Two hours later, I called Pancho to see what the deal was. "Yo Pancho, what it do?"

"Dude's driving a tan Impala with rims on it. He just pulled off. From the description my sister gave me, it's he. I called her and told her to tell him to come to the crib, so the coast is clear."

"So, he gone?"

"Yeah, he gone."

"Juju, you, and Re go up Marquette through the alleyway."

"Why we gotta go through that dark ass alley?"

"Because Tiki and I are going to walk up the street, hop in the car with him, and meet y'all in the alley. I just need y'all to make sure ain't nobody lurking around."

"I guess."

After the final plan was put in motion, Tiki and I walked off to go find Pancho. My bestie and I thought we were on some ninja type shit. We had on all black everything so it was hard for us to be spotted.

BUZZ! BUZZ!

I looked down at my phone and noticed that I had a text message from Pancho. It read, "Black minivan to yo right."

I looked up to my right and saw this fool in an all-black, soccer mom ass van.

"What's the verdict?"

"Third house from the corner. I've only been seeing the dude come and go. He walks through the gangway through the garage. I walked back there to check shit out myself. The garage is raggedy as shit, but the door looks like something you gon have to blow the fuck off the hinges. Steel with a big ass lock on it."

"Let's make this move then."

We drove around to the back of the garage to get a good look for ourselves.

"Damn, how we gon get up in that motha fucker?"

Pancho got out of the van, walked to the back, and popped the door.

"I got these chains to see if we could just pull the door off since the garage is about one gust of wind from blowing the fuck away, anyway."

"My nigga, now you thinking. Hook that shit up and let's get it."

My besties and me all took a few steps back and let this nigga work his magic. I whispered to ReRe, "After we get the bread, I'mma kill Pancho. This shit gon eventually hit the fan. Niggas ain't gon just sit back and accept this type of loss. I don't want nobody coming over here applying pressure to the hood. He can't be trusted, Re. This nigga set up his own fucking cousin. Fuck you think he'll do to us?"

I turned back just in time to see Pancho slowly easing the van forward.

"Don't pull it all the way off."

"I got you."

He pulled a few more feet before I saw the wood start to cracking around the door. The door began to shift as the wood broke away from the frame.

"Alright, stop."

I was the first to enter the garage. Why the fuck did I do that? Next thing you know, I heard all types of growling.

"AWWW SHIT!"

Four big ass pit bulls rushed my ass, knocking me to the floor.

"CODE FOUR! MAN DOWN! MAN DOWN! SHOOT THESE MAFUCKING DOGS!"

Tiki ran in the hoe blazing.

POP! POP! POP! POP!

My bestie a beast! That hoe aim on point. My other two besties ran in there to find me on the floor with my pants to my ankles, my hoodie ripped, and four dead ass dogs surrounding me. These hoes had the nerve to start laughing.

"Fuck y'all laughing at? Hurry up and let's find this money and let's bounce before the police come. I know somebody heard those shots."

There was so much junk in there that I thought we'd be there all night. Luckily it wasn't.

"Tiki, what's them black bags in the corner over there under the table?"

"JACKPOT!"

"Let's get the fuck outta here!"

I had never seen that much money before in my life.

"Okay, Tiki you and JuJu wait thirty seconds after we leave and then y'all take the money and go to Lil Mama's. Wait on my call. Ju, you still got the keys, don't you?"

"Yeah."

"Take the bread over there and chill."

I looked at ReRe. "Re, you ready to make that move?"

It was quiet as fuck outside the garage. "Call Pancho."

Re picked up her phone and placed the call as we walked through the gateway.

"Where you at?" She hung up and said, "He's in the same spot we met him at."

I looked at her for a few seconds before I said, "You know I'm about to shoot this nigga; right?"

She just nodded her head. No words were needed. We hopped in the van and he pulled off. He kept staring at me as if I was crazy.

"Fuck happened to yo clothes?"

This pussy had the nerve to start laughing as if he knew something I didn't. "You got jokes, huh? Why you ain't tell me about them fucking dogs?"

He stopped laughing when he heard the seriousness in my voice. See, motha fuckers in the hood know that by me being a female didn't mean shit. I got a few bodies under my belt.

"Man Joe, I didn't know it was no dogs."

I could see the lie all in his eyes. Too bad that he didn't see his death in mine. "A, go back to the garage and scoop up Ju and Tiki. Them bags heavy as shit."

He pulled around the corner and into the alley. He put the van in park and were the first to hop out and begin walking towards the garage. When he went in, I was right behind his ass.

"Where they at E?"

He turned around to see me pointing my gun in his direction.

"What the fuck you doing? This how you gon get down on me?"

I didn't have time for small talk. "Ain't no room in my hood for snakes. You aren't right and I don't trust yo ass. You probably was planning on killing us, but then again, you too pussy for that. You was going to get somebody to get at us. Not tonight, nigga!"

Sensing that he was about to die, he said some shit to make me think.

"Bitch ass nigga, I ain't slow. I got insurance better than All-State. You kill me and motha fuckers gon come for you; all y'all!" A dead nigga will say anything.

POW! POW!

I shot him once in the stomach, and once in the chest. I knew it was a possibility that he could survive both. Plus, I wanted his hoe ass to suffer a little.

"Man, you ain't gotta do this, E! Com---."

POW!

I painted the garage floor with that niggas brains. Had I done my homework, I wouldn't have hit that lick like that. I knew there was money in the garage, but what I didn't know was that the whole outside area around the garage was surrounded by cameras. I also found out that me, Pancho, and my besties weren't the only ones who knew we were going to take that money. DAMN!

"These hoes ain't loyal
no they ain't!"

$\mathcal{J}_{\mathcal{R}}$ **9**

Ever since my brother, Big Moe, and I hit this last lick, we've been laying low. Boogie's been getting on my fucking nerves too. Every few hours h's calling me, telling me to go check on the bread. He and Big Moe still live up north where the Cabrini Greens building use to be. I moved south to Dolton, Illinois, which is a suburb about ten minutes from the city.

I guess since I'm the one who found the safe spot to rent; I'm the one that has to babysit the money. Ain't that some shit? Even though the spot's in a fucked up neighborhood, the spot is low key. Plus, I installed a few security cameras around the crib. If that's not enough, I got some mean ass pit bulls in the garage guarding the money. In case a mothafucka still want to be nosey, I put "No Bark" collars around their necks. If they bark, those collars are going to shock the fuck out of their asses. Break up in the garage if you want too! My pits gon eat they assess alive.

I rolled through at least two times a day. Once in the morning and once at night before I head to the crib. Like tonight, I'm here making sure everything is cool. I just fed my dogs and I'm on the way back to my car when my phone rings.

"Who is this?"

"That's not the way you suppose to answer yo phone."

I smiled, knowing the identity of the caller. "What up boo?"

"When you coming home? My pussy missing you."

I love how blunt shawty is. "Yeah, I'm about to come through and make yo ass tap out. Be ready when I get there."

"Hurry up boo. I got my hand on your favorite spot right now."

"Oh yeah? Let me hear you moan for me."

Listening to her moan made my dick harder than Chinese arithmetic. I jumped in my car with quickness. I fuck with shawty the long way. Been with her for a couple of months. I'm not like Boogie or Big Moe's crazy asses. I love hard. My G-ma always told me that I was the sensitive one. I got a good heart. I get that from my mama.

She died when Boogie and I were little. Some nigga she was fucking threw her off the roof of the project building where we lived. We were playing on the playground in the front of the building. We actually heard her screams as she fell fifteen stories to the parking lot. Her body crashed through a parked car's windshield.

Boogie stood frozen on the playground. I wanted to go get my mama. My young mind didn't grasp the fact that nobody could survive that fall but superman, and since we have no damn superman in the projects, she had to be dead.

As people were running around screaming for help, I made my way over to get my mama. I thought my mama was alive because we made eye contact as I walked up to her.

"Ma get up. Want me to go get G-ma so she can help make you feel better?"

No answer.

Then I heard my G-ma scream, "MOTHERFUCKA! NOT MY BABY! OH LAWD A MERCY!"

I only then realized that she was gone. Unlike Big Moe's mama who left him, my mama took care of Boogie and me. She loved us. When she died, my G-ma tried to love us the same way. Boogie hung up under Big Moe so he treated women the way Big Moe did. Like shit!

Me on the other hand, I love easily. I know what you're thinking, yeah I set the bank tellers up and then kill they ass. That's different. It's business!

When I meet a chick outside of that bank shit, if we hit it off then we're all good. Luck has it; I met Tutu over East where I got the spot. She said she was visiting some family. I looked at the crib trying to decide if I wanted to rent it. We hit it off and I ended up renting the spot.

Big Moe and Boogie don't like her. They say she looks rachet. How does rachet look? Since they don't chose my pussy for me, I started fucking with shawty.

When I'm not *working*, we lay up, pop X pills, and fuck like jackrabbits. This hoe's pussy is so good, it make me want to dig up my mama and slap the death off of her rotten ass. No lie!

"I'm on my way. I'm about to hit the pill spot and the liquor store."

30 Minutes Later

I get to the crib ready to put that hoe in a coma. I already popped my pill on the way so I'm feeling right. My fucking phone keeps beeping. I got several different beeps for different things. This particular beep is the alarm system from the safe spot. I had it set up to where I could monitor the back of the house and the garage from my phone. It also beeps when the motion sensor is set off.

One night, I drove over there three times. When I got there, there wasn't shit. I'm not doing that shit tonight. I'm about to touch bottom in some good ass pussy, smoke a kush blunt, and call it a night.

I walked into the crib and the sight that I saw almost made me bust a nut on sight.

"Like what you see?"

Shawty was asshole naked with her best friend's head between her legs. "Damn! I didn't know we had company."

She looked at me with the sexist eyes ever and said, "Strip!"

I got up out my clothes so fast; you would have thought I had an onesie on. All that shit fell to the floor at the same time.

"Come here, JR. My friend wanna let you meet the back of her throat."

"Can she deep throat ten inches?"

"Only one way to find out."

The pill had me feeling so good, I walked over to ol' girl on her knees, and accidently poked her in her eye trying to find her mouth.

"Damn, my bad."

She pulled back and started rubbing her eye. She put my dick in her mouth and used her hands to softly caress my balls. My bitch knows what I like. She positioned herself on the edge of the couch, opened her legs, and said, "Eat!"

I sat on the couch laid back and told my girl to ride my face. I put my dick back in ol' girl mouth and enjoyed the warmth of her mouth. Tutu's pussy so damn sweet. I couldn't help but to get lost in heaven. Between licks and slurps, I started my dick talk.

"Damn boo, yo pussy sweet as fuck! Cum for Daddy!"

I looked up at her riding my face and I can see that she wasn't into it as she normally is. Straight up, I know my tongue game is lethal. I could suck a uterus through a baby bottle nipple. Ol' girl sucking my dick so good that my toes get to cracking.

"Aw shit! Wait! Wait! Aw, fuck! I'm about to fucking bust!"

I grabbed her head with my free hand and pushed my hips in the air so I know I'm touching tonsils. I started rotating my hips until I bust long and hard down her throat.

"AWWWW SHIT, GIRL! SUCK IT ALL BITCH! DAMN!"

And that she did. I pushed Tutu off of me and grabbed her by her neck. "Bend the fuck over, bitch!" She did as she was told and I pushed deep inside her tight walls.

"You ready for Daddy to make this pussy talk to me?"

She looked back at me and said, "Make it last forever."

I started off slow, loving the way her juices coated my dick. Her pussy so damn hypnotizing you'd get lost in a zone. I swear! Got a nigga trying to make love. Am I a lame for that? Fuck whoever think so! Ol' girl comes beside me and cocks her leg up on the side of the couch. She looked me dead in the eyes and she started playing with her pussy. "DAMN!"

Now that shit turned me the fuck on. "Let's cum together," she said.

I started digging in Tutu's pussy like I loss something and was trying my hardest to find it. Although I was enjoying this little freak show shit, something in my gut told me that something was wrong with this picture.

Here I was serving Tutu with some A-one beefcake. I mean, I was deep sea diving in that motha fucker, but this hoe is barely acknowledging my gangsta. I guess she thought I was too high off of them X pills to pay attention to my surroundings, but I wasn't. I was fully aware that instead of enjoying this dick, this bitch would rather fidget with her phone.

"Damn Tutu! Throw that pussy back! Fuck wrong with you?"

Sensing that I was about to get mad and act a fucking fool, she started doing that thing I like when she squeezes her pussy muscles and rotates her ass around.

"Yeah, get that shit girl."

Now I'm really trying to bust a nut before I choke slam this bitch. As I'm pounding away, I could see her phone light popping on and off. It did that like three times. What the fuck? Thinking that it's probably another nigga, I got ready to beat that hoe's ass.

"Man Joe, suck dick!"

I pulled out and snatched her up by her hair.

"Baby, let me ride you."

I looked back at her friend and back at her. "Naw, suck her pussy while she sucks my dick."

She looked like she wanted to say something until she saw the murderous look on my face.

"Fuck you waiting for?"

As she got on her knees to pleasure her friend, I let ol' girls mouth take me to heaven. This bitch had a grip tighter than Poly Grip. I nutted in her mouth in no time. Since I was finished, I guess Tutu thought she was too.

"Where you on yo way to? I'm about to go wash up."

I looked at ol' girl. "Did you cum, shawty?" She smiled at me and said, "Almost."

I looked at Tutu and said, "Almost doesn't count. Finish what you started."

She looked at the both of us with that, *I Hate You* look. I didn't give a fuck, because if that was a nigga blowing up her phone, I'mma blow her fucking brains out!

After about five minutes, ol' girl finally got her nut.

"Go get in the shower and wait for me."

She went to grab her phone and walk off. "Bitch, you don't need no phone to shower. Put that motha fucker down before I break that bitch."

She reluctantly put her phone on the table and walked to the bathroom. I went in my pockets and pulled out five one hundred dollar bills. "Let me get 'cha number, Joe. I'mma get at you again. Yo shit on point, baby girl."

She gave me her number and before she left, she turned to me and said, "Be careful. Everybody ain't who you think they are."

I wanted to ask her what she meant, but I took it as my girl was cheating on me and she was dry snitching on her ass. These hoes aren't loyal! I went straight to the bathroom and hopped in the shower with Tutu. I grabbed her by the arm and turned her around so that I could look in her eyes. When I did that, I saw tears streaming down her face.

"Why you crying? You cheating on me, Tutu?"

She looked at me with a shocked look on her face. "No, I'm not cheating on you."

I stared at my chick for a few minutes. On some real shit, she looked like she was telling the truth. I still couldn't shake that feeling that something just wasn't right.

I fucked her in every room in the house ending back in the living room.

"Tutu, I love you."

"I love you too. Go to sleep."

Her ass left me awake by myself so I flamed up my kush blunt, turned on ESPN, and watched the highlights from the Bulls and Heat game. My nigga D-Rose showed the fuck out beating the Heat by sixteen points.

In the back of my mind, I still couldn't shake that feeling that something wasn't right. I blame it on them pills. "I gotta stop popping those fucking pills."

I put the blunt in the ashtray and readied to lay it down with my boo when I saw her phone light up on the table. I walk over to the table and pick the phone up. She had eight text messages. I grabbed the blunt out the ashtray and opened her messages.

"Who the fuck is Pancho?"

There were about thirty messages back and forth between their asses. As I read the messages, I got mad all over again. I couldn't believe what I was reading. "This grimy ass bitch! She never even told me she even had a brother."

I got to the last five messages and my heart began racing. This one message got me on murder mode. It read, *"Pancho, get yo crew together. The money at 8514 Marquette in the garage. Be careful he got four pit bulls and cameras around the garage."*

"Oh yeah?"

I kept reading. The next text was sent earlier tonight.

"I'mma get him high. Make sure you get every dime!"

I read the text he sent and it said, *"I'll call you when I kill 'em."*

I grabbed my phone from my pants pocket. I had sixteen alerts from my security setup. My heart dropped to the pit of my stomach when I played the video. What I saw changed every good bone I had in my body for this bitch. After seeing that video, I had murder on my mind and this bitch was the number one victim.

I walk over to where she was sleeping. "Wake up shawty. Come on, we gotta take a ride real quick."

"What's wrong, boo?"

"My alarm is going off at the spot."

I watched her go into a state of panic. "What alarm?"

Then she hit me with, "Baby my pussy is on swole. You wore me out. Let's go in the morning. It's probably nothing."

I wanted to shoot this hoe in her lying ass mouth. "Get the fuck up. Don't make me ask you again."

As she reluctantly got up and started dressing, I sat on the edge of the couch and watched her fidget. "What you looking all crazy for?"

"I'm just tired."

Tired my ass, I thought. Ten minutes later, we were on the expressway.

"Why you so quiet?"

I looked at her and watched her bite her nails, something she did when she was nervous. I couldn't take it anymore.

"Damn Tutu, why?"

She looked at me with tears in her eyes, "I never meant to hurt you."

WHACK!

I smacked her so hard that her head bounced off the window. I didn't say another word as we got off on 87th Street. When I finally pulled around the back of the house to where the garage was, I could see the door pulled halfway off.

"Bitch, get the fuck out!" I snatched that bitch out through the driver's side door.

"Call Pancho!" I handed her, her phone. She looked like she wanted to pass out.

"Yeah bitch, I read every text."

I hawked up and spit in her face.

"You a snake ass hoe!"

She silently cried as she dialed his number. It kept going to voicemail.

"Keep calling!"

I walked to the door to peek inside. "Come here."

I saw all my fucking dogs dead on the ground with a body laid in the middle of them. I walked towards the body to see if my dogs ate this nigga up. I bent down to see all this nigga's brains on the floor.

"Who the fuck--."

"OH NOOOOOOO! PANCHO! NO! NO! NO!"

Tutu came running into the garage damn near knocking me over. She fell to the ground pulling at the dead body.

"PANCHO! PLEASE GET UP!"

She was screaming so loud that I know God heard her. Had she not set me up, I would have felt bad for the bitch. I pulled out my gun and pointed it to the back of her head. "Bitch you don't have to cry. You bout to go where this nigga went."

"JR please... I know I fucked up, but please don't kill me. You don't have to fuck with me. I won't say shit to nobody."

I looked at this hoe as if she was crazy. "Bitch, I gotta answer to my crazy ass cousin who thought you wasn't shit to begin with. How the fuck am I gonna explain $345,000.00 missing?"

I wanted to kill this bitch so bad, but truth be told, I was in love with this ol' conniving ass bitch.

"Tell me why I shouldn't kill you."

"Because I know who did this."

RING! RING!

I snatched the phone from her hand and saw that Pancho's number was on the screen.

"Who dis?"

The caller was real bold. "Fuck you and that snake ass nigga, Pancho!"

*"Go shawty, it's yo birthday, we gon party
like it's yo birthday, and you know we don't
give a fuck cuz it's yo birthday!"*

ju ju 10

One Week Later

I thought having that money would make me feel
better. We split it four ways. Each of us came off
with $91,250.00 apiece. That lick couldn't have
come at a better tie because all our birthdays is this
week. Turn Up!

After we hit the garage, we met up at Lil
Mama's crib. It took E and ReRe forever to get
there and when they finally came, they were on
some silent shit. I'm not slow. I knew E was going

to kill Pancho. I felt that shit coming a mile away. That nigga couldn't be trusted anyway so, fuck 'em.

I do know that this money is not going to last forever. That robbery gave me a new burst of energy. Knowing that this money is from a bank that was robbed, I started to think. We can take a bank, hands down. If it's money like this in a bank, all we need to do is hit like one or two and we'd be set for a minute.

Easier said than done. I'll find a way to hip my besties and see what they got to say. Today we bout to hit up Indiana and snatch us a few cars.

RING! RING!

I grabbed my phone and saw that it's my boo, LJ. I haven't really spoken to him since the robbery.

"What's up, sexy? You miss me?"

I was smiling harder than a fat bitch pulling up to McDonald's. "Hey back at you handsome. Yes I miss you."

"I can't tell. I haven't heard from yo ass in a few days. Where you at?"

"I'm bout to get up with the besties and we're bout to hit a few car lots in Indiana."

"You bout to get a whip?"

"Yeah."

"Why you ain't hit me up?"

"I dunno. I just thought I'd roll up on you when I got my shit."

"How much you trying to spend?"

Now see, why does he need to get all in my business like that? I hate lying to him about my business, but it's just that, my business.

"My auntie gave me a few thousand. You know a going back to school present."

"Alright, that's cool, but you should let me and Poohman take y'all so y'all don't get scammed by a shady ass car salesman named Bob."

I got out the bed and headed for the shower.

"Come on."

E

I'm tripping the fuck out right now. I don't know how I'm going to explain this to my besties without them flipping the fuck out, Ju in particular. I'm glad I killed that pussy ass nigga, Pancho. That nigga was not to be trusted. I knew he was going to try and double cross us. This clown ass nigga even had the nerve to text some hoe named Tutu saying that he would call her after he killed us. The nerve of this nigga.

Now I need to figure out who this hoe is. Wait a minute; I'm on some slow shit. Tutu that nigga's sister. Does she even know that this nigga's dead? She's been calling and texting his phone all day and night. I called it back a few nights ago. Some clown talking about, "Who dis?"

She must know that he's dead because it was her name that popped up on the screen. The nigga must have been JR. For now, fuck that bitch and her dead ass brother. It's our birthday week and we're about to get it in. We're about to go cop us some whips and hit the malls.

*"Y'all need to move da doe, y'all need
to move da doe, move da doe, ay move
da doe, y'all need to move da doe!"*

ℒℊ 11

"**Y**o Poohman, come make this move with
me real quick. I'm taking JuJu and her
little crew out to Indiana to get some whips."

He laughed.

"What's so funny, bro?"

"He said that they all was gonna go get them a
car. I asked her where she got the money from -."

"And let me guess, she said from Ju's auntie, Lil
Mama, right?"

"Bingo."

I trust shawty because she bout that life. I really don't want to think that she would lie to me about shit because she don't have to. Her auntie did just do a bid for bank robbery. I know she put some bread away because my auntie Boo told me.

"Ju, I'm on my way."

30 Minutes Later

"Poohman, yo ass crazy as shit, boy. So, let me get this straight. You had a crush on Pam Grier when you was a shawty?"

"Hell yeah! If I was old enough back then, I would have took her ass down."

I'm choking on this weed smoke. "Would you hit now, my nigga?"

"Hell naw! She old as fuck now. Plus, she fat as shit. You know I don't do fat hoes."

I'm laughing so hard that I've got tears coming out of my eyes.

"Ay, pull over in the gas station, nigga, I need some gum."

"Yo ass need some help!" I pulled over at the Citgo on 79th and Yates. "Poohman put forty-five on pump five."

This cheap ass nigga walked over to me and put his hand out.

"What nigga?"

He gon look at me as if I'm in the wrong. "Man Joe, give me half."

I went in my pockets shaking my head. "Cheap ass!"

"Whatever!"

I put the pump in the tank and waited for it to begin pumping. I heard somebody's car knocking off the chain. Whoever that is has some serious bass in their trunk.

"God damn!"

They weren't even in the gas station and I heard their shit loud and clear. Next thing you know, this tan Impala whips up to the pump next to me. Dude's shit was beating so loud that he has my windows shaking. He's got some nice ass rims on his shit too. His shit isn't fucking with mine, but he can pull some hoes.

"Jaw, what up nigga?"

I turned around to see my nigga JR. I grew up with this nigga. His uncle used to run with my uncle in the projects.

"JR, what yo black ass doing on this side of town? You a long way from the Greens."

I looked into his eyes and I can see the stress all over his face.

"You good, my nigga?"

"Hell naw! I got a little spot over on 85th and Marquette. Last night a motha fucker stained me for three hundred fifty G's."

I almost passed out.

"And that ain't even the worst part. That money belonged to me, Boogie, and Big Moe!"

"Damn Joe! That's fucked up! That nigga still crazy?"

"Hell yeah, but the killing part of the whole situation is that the little hoe I'm fucking is the one that set me up to get hit!"

"Damn, my nigga! Yo ass got problems!"

"The good side of it is that she told me who helped her brother steal my shit."

"Wait! Her brother? Where that nigga at?"

"When I went to check on the money, dude ass was laying in the middle of the garage, dead!"

"So the niggas that helped him hit the lick killed his ass afterwards?"

"Yeah. She said it was four niggas. She only know one of their names. Some dude named, Dirty E."

I had a bad taste in my mouth. "Ay Joe, is Dirty E a nigga?"

"Yeah. Why?"

"No reason."

I took a deep breath. For some reason I thought about my boo and her little crew. They don't even look like they get down like that.

"Here go my number. Hit me if you need me."

I see Poohman coming out the gas station with a mug on his face. JR and Poohman never saw eye-to-eye. They even fist fought a couple of times.

Poohman always got the best of JR until Boogie jumped in and that's when I jumped in. It was all love with JR and Boogie. I didn't fuck with Big Moe like that. He was a nut. Poohman didn't fuck with Big Moe either.

JR looked at Poohman and smiled, "What up Pooh?"

"Fuck you nigga!"

"Damn dawg, you still mad?"

"Hell naw, nigga! You can't whoop me by yo'self, pussy."

Let me end this shit before these two niggas send this gas station up. "Alright JR, holla at me if you need me."

I hopped back in my car and peeled off. "Call Re and tell them we on the way."

While Poohman called the girls, I couldn't help but think about what JR told me.

"What you thinking about?"

I told him all of what JR said.

"My first thought was the girls. I dismissed that shit because I just can't see them getting down like that; feel me?"

We spent the rest of the day helping the girls pick out cars. I was impressed at my boo's taste. She chose this money green; two door ninety-six Cutlass. Straight throw back! The interior had peanut butter colored leather. It had a sunroof and the miles were really low. The funny thing is that all of them chose Cutties.

ReRe chose this all-black drop top Cutlass. I think it was a ninety-five. The inside was sick. White leather, my nigga! Tiki chose this four door white Cutlass with white leather. It had a roof, too. Man Joe, Dirty killed the game when she copped a red two door Coupe with red and black racecar seats. The windows were tinted red.

Poohman and I helped with the tags and insurance since their young ass didn't have a license. JuJu walked towards me talking a mile a minute.

"Boo, we gotta hit the rim and sound store. I wanna get four, twelve's in the trunk and I want twenty-tow inch rims."

"You don't even have an alarm. Slow down, I got you."

"Oooh and we gotta get some customized plates that say E.S.C."

"What that mean?"

She smiled at me with joy in her eyes. "Eastside Crazy!"

Poohman and I looked at each other and I walked towards my car to grab my phone.

"Where you going, boo?"

"I gotta make a phone call, shawty."

"Went to sleep real, woke up realer,
Goon affiliated, ex drug dealer, resume`
solid, street cred bigger!"

Auntie Boo 12

"What up, nephew? Huh? How much you say she gave them? I dunno about all that, but I'll get to the bottom of it and I'mma hit you later."

I hear shit in the streets, but I'mma vet. I don't believe everything I hear. My nephew has been spending time with my Goddaughter JuJu for a month or so. I see that he likes her. Some things came to light and it got him concerned. So what does he do? He calls me because I get to the bottom of EVERYTHING!

First, he says that she always has money. We all know her little bad ass doesn't have a job and her little friends don't either. This hood been in an uproar since they found Pancho's body on the next block dead in some garage. Rumor has it; he was robbed and then murdered.

Come to think of it, for the last year or so, all these little dough boys around here have been getting robbed. I also heard that Pancho had a hand in each and every robbery. There's no telling who killed his shiesty ass.

Jaw asked me to ask Lil Mama if she gave JuJu and her little besties some money because they had a few thousand apiece and they all said that Lil Mama gave it to them. I know the answer to that already. HELL NAW! I know she does for them here and there, but not a few thousand apiece. Something is going on and I'm the one that's going to find out.

I know that they're not fucking, so tricking is out of the question. I really don't want to call Lil Mama and get her all in an uproar. She doesn't play with JuJu and she damn sure doesn't play about her. She loves that girl like a daughter.

What most don't know because we don't talk about it is that Lil Mama and Ja`ziya's mother Lil Baby were identical twins. Lil Baby had JuJu and then hit the streets. She chased that almighty dollar until her feet were sore. Ju always knew the difference, but Lil Mama was always there.

After Lil Mama finished high school, she hit the streets too. She kept her niece with her until she started hitting banks. She paid her younger sister, Shante' to watch her.

Things went left and quiet as kept; Tae was the reason that she got popped by the FEDS. She was out drinking one night and she got loose with her mouth. Somebody turned Lil Mama in for that reward money. She left her stash with me. She only left Tae with enough to take care of JuJu. She knew Tae wasn't going to take care of her, so I did.

Now they don't fuck with each other at all. Hell, Ja`ziya barely stays with Tae now that Lil Mama is home. I can't figure this shit out. Let me call Lil

Mama and let her know what's going on. If I keep this from her, this crazy ass Jamaican is going to have a fit! I don't feel like fighting that hoe, nor do I care to be called all these blood clots and bumba clots. I don't even know what that shit mean. I do know that it isn't nice.

"Hey hoe, what you doing? What? Wait kill who? JuJu? Why? WHAT? I'm on the way!"

Lil Mama

I'm so mad that I can't even see straight. Here I am, trying to be all domesticated and shit, cleaning up after this funky ass niece of mine. I don't snoop through her shit because I was in prison for almost eight years. The correctional officers always went through our things. That shit is degrading and most of it is unnecessary.

They went as far as throwing our clean clothes on the floor. Spilling food on them and even allowing the K9's to walk on our clean beds. Their dirty asses would leave our lockers open and other inmates would steal our shit. I never want her to feel like she don't have privacy in my house because she does.

I know the last eight years have been rough on her. My sister didn't treat her right, so that's why I gave her that privacy and fresh air to breathe. This little heifer and her *besties* as she would call them, leaves this room a damn mess, so I call myself being nice and cleaning this room. As I'm picking up the clean clothes and putting them back in the closet where they belong, I find a black bag full of money.

"What the fuck?"

I sat there and counted the money. I almost blew a fuse, y'all! This bitch has nearly $350,000.00 in there. It was separated into four different bundles. Then I thought, four bundles, four girls. I'mma kill this little girl!

15 Minutes Later

KNOCK! KNOCK!

"Boo, it's open."

My best friend walks in to find me sitting on JuJu's closet floor.

"How much you find?"

I shook my head and said, "It's more than my stash."

She gave me that, "*Damn*" look.

"Boo, these damn kids done did some shit that got some serious consequences behind it. I know they must be holding this for somebody. I know they're little scary asses ain't out here making moves like this."

Boo sat down next to me. "Don't trip sis, we gon find out what's going on. Let me find out yo ass paranoid."

"Hell naw, hoe! I am not paranoid! I'm on parole!"

*"All I talk about is money, cuz
that's all I know, ya heard me!"*

Big Moe 13

"Hello."

"Big Moe."

"What nigga?"

"We got a problem."

"It better not involve my money!"

"Meet me over East."

I had a feeling that I was going to murder me a motha fucker today. I just didn't think it would be my own blood. Something told me to just grab my share of that money.

I jumped up and hit the showers real quick. Thirty minutes later, I'm out the door. Damn, it's a nice day. I had plans to chill, too bad I'm about to make the city rain red today. I'm cruising down 79th. The hoes are out.

"Damn, who is that?" I had to pull over. Shawty was a redbone and she was thick to death. I need some new pussy in my life. I pull up in the parking lot to this laundry mat on 79th and Colfax. I hopped out and went up to a corner store looking for the ol' girl.

"A, you seen shawty that just came in here?"

The cashier points to the back of the store. I walk back there and I see her at the counter ordering some steaks. "You gon cook one for me"

She turns around and gives me this, *who the fuck are you look.*

"A, whatever she buying, I'm paying for."

"Naw, I'm good. Thanks anyway."

She turned around, grabbed her food, and handed the clerk a fifty. "This should cover my bill and whatever I'm getting." She looked at me, smiled, and walked off.

"Damn!" I told the clerk to give me her change and I ran after her. Yes, I ran. Shawty was that bad! I get to the front of the store just in time to see her on her phone.

"Let me get the number to that phone, so I can call you."

She ended her call and then asked, "Is that how you try and holla at a female? If so, then yo ass need lessons."

The nerve of this bitch! She's fine, but I'll slap the fuck out this hoe. I'm just trying to fuck. Now I'mma make her suck my dick too! Smart-ass mouth. "I don't mean no disrespect. You bad! What else can I say?"

She cracks a smile. "You shoulda just said that then. I'm Boo."

JR

"Tutu, I think you should leave before Big Moe gets here."

She jumped out the bed so fast; you would have thought it was on fire. "I agree, baby."

I beat the shit outta her for getting me robbed. I really do love this hoe. Anybody else would be floating in Lake Michigan. Plus, I think losing her brother was torture enough.

"Why you think you having a free day, bitch? You better go over East and find out who the fuck them niggas is before I stomp yo face into the ground, bitch!"

Tutu

I'm sitting in the bed watching TV when JR comes and tells me that I should leave before his cousin gets here. That shit was like music to my ears. Since Pancho died, he's been beating me one minute, and then fucking me the next. I do need some air, plus I'm going to find out who the fuck killed my brother.

After I hopped out of the shower, I called my little brother.

"Hello."

"What up, Tutu? Where you been?"

"I'm on my way over there. Where you at?"

"I'm at home."

"Lil Man, don't tell nobody I'm coming, ok? I wanna holla at you about Pancho, ok."

"Okay."

I walk in the living room on my way out the door and I see JR looking out the window.

"Big Moe here."

Big Moe

"Boogie, I'm at JR's crib, come through."

"Alright, give me about forty-five minutes."

I hope this nigga tells me something good. As I make my way up to the front door, his trifling ass bitch, Tutu is coming out.

"Hey, Big Moe."

"What up? Where JR?"

"In the living room waiting on you."

Every time I see her, I get a bad feeling about her. I told JR, but the nigga is too pussy-whipped. Ol' sucka ass nigga!

"What up, JR?"

"Man Joe, somebody hit the spot."

I knew that shit was coming so I didn't even snap off the bat. Deep down inside, I knew that he would never cross me, but something isn't right. He played the security video for me.

"So, it was five of them?"

"It's four now. Dude in the white tee was dead in the garage with my damn dogs. He don't look familiar."

I had to ask him. "Where was yo bitch at?"

He shook his head and chuckled. "She was here with me, cuz."

"So what now, my nigga? I'm not about to take a loss like that. Somebody gon pay for this shit! In the meantime, we got another job at a Chase Bank in Hammond Indiana. I was told the payout could

be up to half a ticket. So get cha mind right;
alright?"

"Where's Boogie?"

"He's on his way so we can go over the details."

"Somebody who you're around wants to clip your wings and shoot ya down, but it's okay to keep enemies close, as long as you know who you're around!"

ℒℐ 14

I'm on the way to scoop up Poohman so that we can chop it up as to what my Auntie Boo told me about JuJu and her damn besties. As I pulled up to his house, I see JR's car in front of his crib.

"What the hell he doing over this way?"

I hop out my whip and walked over to the driver side window. It slides down "What up my --. Oh my bad shawty, I thought you was somebody else."

She licks her lips and smiles. "I can be whoever you want me to be."

These hoes will do anything. "Ain't this JR's car?"

The sound of his name wiped that smile clean off her face.

"Be easy."

Poohman comes out the house arguing with somebody on the phone. "Don't make me come fuck you up, shawty. What? We need a break? You tripping! Holla at me when you get yo mind right."

He hung up the phone and looked at me. "ReRe just told me she needs some time."

I fell out laughing. I relayed what Boo told me.

"Poohman, the little ass up to something and I got a feeling that we going to have to pull them burners out."

JuJu

Our birthday weekend was the fucking greatest! We had so much fun hitting up Great America. Tiki was on the sad side, but we got her through it. We hit the Mall of America in Minnesota. All together, we spent forty G's. I don't know, but I think LJ is in his feelings about something. He's been real quiet lately.

After our birthday week, we all sat down and had a long talk about our next lick. Since E made Pancho take that dirt nap, her ass was in charge of setting up things.

"So, I was thinking about hitting a bank."

They all looked at me as if I was crazy. Re smiled at me and said, "That's what the fuck I'm talking about."

I looked at ReRe and said, "I know we got this. All we gotta do is find a spot and case it."

I was talking as if I knew what the fuck to do. E spoke up, "I read about a case outside of Harvey, Illinois, where these four dudes got away with $400,000.00. They watched the bank manager, followed her home, and got her there. Two people stayed back watching the house, and the other two took her back to the bank and got the money. Simple, right?"

We all sat around in silence for a few minute. Tiki broke the silence, "We can case the bank for at least a week, learn the routines, and go from there."

Deep down I was scared as shit, but excited at the same time.

"Alright, when we start?"

E and Tiki looked at me and smiled. "Me and Tiki already did. We gon hit the Chase Bank in Hammond, Indiana."

I was curious now. "How y'all even come up with this shit?"

ReRe looked at me and said, "We passed it on the way to get our whips. It's off in the cut and the expressway is less than a mile from the bank."

I looked at ReRe with steam coming from my ears. "Why y'all keep that shit from me, though?"

E shook her head, "Because you been caking with ya boo and we wanted to make sure things were right before we let you know. You know yo ass is crazy, Ju!"

I had to smile because they know me. If shit isn't right, I will blank the fuck out! I looked at ReRe. "What you gon tell Poohman? You know he be on your bumper."

"I already told him that I need some me time."

I started laughing because LJ isn't going for that shit. He's already acting funny because I don't ask him for shit. I don't want his dope money. To be honest, I hate drug dealers and their money. He isn't too flashy and he doesn't have a gang of hoes in his face. I want to be with him, but I want my own bread.

"E, when we doing this?"

"In two days."

"Alright, let me put some space in between me and Jaw."

LJ

"Hello. What up sexy?"

"Hey."

"What's wrong with you?"

"You know I fucks with you the long way, right?"

"What's on yo mind, shawty?"

"I'mma fall back off you for a minute. I need to get my shit right."

"What shit, Ju?"

"I just got some things to iron out, okay?"

"Man whatever, shawty!"

I hung up on her before I ended up cursing her punk ass out. What the fuck is going on with them damn girls? Poohman and I have been on our detective shit. Hell yeah, you heard me right. We've been following their asses. Ju hasn't been on shit, but the other three been real busy taking trips to Indiana every day.

When we followed them yesterday, I told Poohman to call his girl just to see if she would lie about where they were.

"What up shawty? Where you at? Oh yeah, when she gon be finish doing yo hair? Just checking on you. Hit me when you done."

I looked at Poohman and shook my head. "Something ain't right, bro."

Big Moe

The next bank job was my doing. I met this chick name Andrea at the Horseshoe Casino last week. She was sexy as fuck, I must admit. We chopped it up for the rest of the night and before dawn; I had her touching her ankles in her apartment. Come to find out, she was a bank manager for a Chase Bank in Hammond, Indiana. BINGO!

So for the last week, I've been dicking down this hoe. Her pussy is some A-One Platinum shit, too. It's a damn shame, I'mma kill her once the job is done. From what she said, we could walk away with more than a half a million. The reason why this bank is holding so much money is because it deals with the casino and their payouts on a regular basis. We need that!

Don't get shit twisted. I'm still on the hunt for that $350,000.00. I'm not about to accept that kind of loss without a few bodies dropping. I do know that something isn't right with my little cuz, JR. I think he knows more than he's saying. Only time will tell. For now, I'mma let it be. We need to focus on this job that is coming up.

Speaking of focusing, I've been chatting with this chick Boo. Shawty got my attention and that's a first. She a few years older than me. On some real shit, I swear I know her from somewhere.

When I'm not fucking Andrea into La-La Land, I'm kicking the bobo with Boo.

After we hit this last lick, I'mma chill for a while. Plan some new shit and change up our M.O.

*"Yep, I want the money, cars, and the
clothes, clothes and the hoes, I suppose.
I just wanna be, I just wanna be successful!"*

Dirty & 15

"Okay, the final plans are in motion. We can't fuck this up y'all!"

I looked around the room at my besties. My ride or die bitches. What we're about to do today will forever change our lives.

"JuJu, you and Tiki will go to the bank manager's house and wait for my call. Me and ReRe are going to run up in the bank. ReRe, we in and out in three minutes, no matter what. She gets there every morning at 7 a.m. sharp. We gon take her at the door. Any questions?"

Ju raised her hand. "We going to the house, for what? I want to be close in case y'all need us. I'm not scared to bust this .380."

I smiled at JuJu. "I know, but if she doesn't comply, then we gon need y'all to snatch her kids up. They get on the school bus every morning at five after seven. Y'all, we got this! I looked at my watch, "Come on, it's 6:30. Let's move out!"

Big Moe

"So, my niggas, it's simple. We going in there at five after seven. That'll give her time to disarm the alarm and get to the vault. Boogie, you hit the vault. JR, you watch his back and watch the front door. I'mma get shawty in her office. Boogie, you make sure y'all get every dime. She said it should take like ten minutes to load all that money. Cut that shit to five! No fuck ups! Any questions?"

I checked the time and it was 6:45. "Let's roll!"

LJ

Call me a stalker if you want. I don't give a fuck. My bitch has been acting funny and I want to know why. Poohman and I have been following these little motha fuckers for over a week now. I got the giggles like shit because from what we've been seeing, it looks like these motha fuckers are planning on robbing a bank. I wanted to see how their little asses were, so Poohman and I were going to lay in the cut and watch.

"A, my nigga, they just left. Wake yo ass up." I punched Poohman's leg.

This goofy ass nigga is going to look at me and smile, "Our bitches been watching too much *Set It Off*."

"It's time to hit, my dude. It's 6:50. Let's get there and post up. I wanna see this shit."

JuJu 6:59 a.m.

"E, we here." I hung up the phone with so many thoughts in my head. Robbery, kidnapping, and some mo shit. If we get caught, we going down.

"Ju quit biting yo nails."

I looked at Tiki and smiled, "My nigga, I just want us to be okay."

She grabbed my hand from my mouth. "We got this. Ain't shit gon go wrong."

Dirty E 7:02 a.m.

"Re, there she go. You ready?"

We walked towards the lady while holding hands. To the average person, we looked like a happy couple. "E, walk ahead right now. She put the key in the door."

I let go of her hand and hit a light sprint just in time to catch her as she unlocked the door.

"Disarm the alarm. If you make a scene, my homies are going to kill them brats you love so much. Don't you live at 9 Roselawn Street?"

Her eyes almost fell out of her head when I said that. "Ple- Please, don't hurt me. I'll do whatever you want."

ReRe walked in behind us. "Open the vault."

LJ 7:03 a.m.

Poohman and I sat watching with our mouths to the floor. We couldn't believe what we were seeing. "Poohman, look at this shit. There goes ya girl walking in the door behind Dirty and that bitch."

Poohman had this unreadable expression on his face. "Jaw, what the fuck?" That was all he could say.

"Where the fuck is Ju and Tiki?"

Big Moe 7:05a.m.

When we made it to the bank, I parked right in front of the spot. I saw Andrea's car so I knew that she was getting shit ready for me.

"Y'all ready?"

Boogie and JR said "yeah" at the same time.

"Let's make this shit quick."

Dirty E 7:07a.m.

"Bitch, help put this money in the bag before I shoot yo ass." That sparked something in her ass, because she started throwing money in the bag as if she was a cashier at a grocery store. She didn't look scared, though.

"When y'all finish, tie me up, and leave through the back door."

I looked at her as if she was crazy. "What?"

Big Moe 7:08a.m.

We could hear voices as we approached the bank offices where she said the vault would be.

"Bitch, help put this money in the bag before I shoot yo ass."

I looked back at my cousins and whispered, "This hoe, set us up."

I pulled out my Glock-40 and walked to where I heard the voices. "Oh yeah Andrea? Bitch, you let another motha fucker hit our lick?"

She looked at the two motha fuckers that held her at gunpoint. "You didn't send them?"

I smacked fire from her ass. "Bitch, I told you, I was gonna do it!"

I looked at this yellow motha fucker holding the gun. "My nigga, this our lick. Y'all can leave or die!"

This a bold motha fucker because he looked me square in the eyes and said, "Then I guess we all about to die, pussy!"

Before I could get another word out, the other gunman drew out of his pants a big ass AK-47. "GET THE FUCK BACK!" Now that was a girl's voice, all day long.

Boogie and JR both pulled out their guns and pointed them at these two gunmen. The one holding the rifle told us, "Y'all got us fucked up!"

LJ 7:08 a.m.

"Poohman, who them three niggas? Wait! Aw, shit! Nigga, ain't that Big Moe, JR, and Boogie?"

He sat up in his seat and looked at me. "My nigga, this bout to get real ugly! Let's go in there! You know them niggas kill onsite!"

I checked my Glock. "Damn, we gon have to kill em all!"

Poohman looked like, "Oh well."

JuJu   7:10 a.m.

Every minute felt like an eternity. "Something ain't right, Tiki. E said in and out in three minutes. It's been seven extra minutes unaccounted for. Call em."

She dialed the number and got no answer.

"Fuck this! Let's go get them!"

The whole ride there I'm thinking, *"Lord, please let them be okay."*

We got to the bank and it looked deserted. "Come on Tiki; let's go see what's good." We checked our guns and were at the front door in a matter of seconds.

ReRe 7:11a.m.

"Y'all niggas better back up before I start shooting."

I don't know who these niggas think they are, but this our lick. I looked at the guy, the manager called Big Moe. "You think I'm playing, nigga?"

CLICK! CLACK!

I popped one in the chamber thinking that would back his ass down. He looked at me and said, "You better kill me, bitch!"

LJ 7:13a.m.

As we crept through the lobby of the bank, I could hear voices coming from the back. Poohman stopped dead in his tracks when he heard ReRe's voice clearly say, "Y'all niggas better back the fuck up before I start shooting!"

I almost fell out laughing because her ass sounded gangsta. Man Joe, when we hit that corner, ReRe's crazy ass was pointing this big ass AK-47 at Big Moe, Boogie, and JR. Poohman was the first to point his gun at them niggas.

"Fuck going on here?"

Even though their faces were partially covered, I could tell it was E and Re. Shit, Re looked like she was about to shoot us too. She looked at E and said, "Bestie, grab them bags and let's go."

She started backing up to the back door. "If y'all niggas want it, I'll murk all y'all! Try me!"

Big Moe wasn't trying to let that money leave that bank. "Shawty, you don't know who you fucking with --."

Before he could finish his statement...

TAT! TAT! TAT!

We all looked on in shock as the bank manager's brains flew from the back of her head. ReRe pointed the gun back at them and said, "Run up!"

JuJu 7:14 a.m.

I heard what sounded like gunshots. Tiki and I flew through that lobby. As we hit the corner, we heard Re loud and clear tell somebody to run up, "Tiki, you ready?"

She was the first to hit the corner, gun pointed. "What the fuck?"

I was on her bumper when she hit the corner. I almost passed out when I saw Jaw and Poohman standing there with their guns pointed at three other niggas. Fuck the fact that there was a dead bitch on the floor. Jaw gave me a look that could have made the devil tuck his tail.

ReRe snapped me out of my trance. "Besties grab that money and let's go!"

I went to grab one of the bags that was on the floor and out of nowhere; one of the dudes went to grab me.

POP! POP!

I closed my eyes and shot. When I finally opened my eyes, dude was on the floor. I knew he was dead. The bullet between his eyes told me so.

Big Moe 7:15a.m.

This shit is outta control. Now here come two mo niggas. More bodies to drop. I looked at Boogie and gave him that familiar nod. When this little nigga attempted to grab, Boogie lunged at him.

POP! POP!

"What the fuck?" My cousin hit the floor hard.

"Boogie, man Joe, get up! Get up!"

I jumped to my feet and started shooting. We're going to blame me missing my targets on the fact that they just fucked my head up by murking my cousin.

Motha fuckers were running in every direction trying not to catch a bullet. JR wasn't even shooting. He was on the ground acting a fool!

"BRO PLEASE GET UP! AWWW, SHIT! MY NIGGA, PLEASE DON'T LEAVE!" He was screaming so loud that I'm sure Boogie's ass heard him in hell.

"Come on cuz, we gotta go! Get up! He dead, nigga! We gotta go before the police come!" I turned and ran in the security room to get the tapes because none of us had on masks. After I got the tapes, I ran and grabbed JR. "Come on baby boy, we gotta go now!"

He looked at me with the saddest eyes ever and said, "I'm killing everything moving until I find out who did this!"

Dude with the dreads sounded very familiar.

"We gon end up on *The First 48*, if we don't dip now! Don't worry, it's on!"

"Many men wish death upon me, blood in eyes dog and I can't see, I'm trying to be what I'm destine to be and niggas trying to take my life away!"

ℒℐ 16

fter that nigga clicked out and started shooting wildly, we all got ghost. I even grabbed one of the bags that was on the floor as we ran out that bitch. I snatched JuJu's arm and Poohman grabbed ReRe's. I told E and Tiki to meet us at my crib. We drove in silence for what seemed like forever. That shit was crazy!

"Ju, you cool?"

She looked at me with this blank ass expression. "Damn, I didn't mean to kill him, boo."

ReRe's crazy ass came out of nowhere. "Fuck them niggas! If you didn't shoot first, guaranteed you'd be the one with the bullet between yo eyes."

Poohman and I made eye contact. Re's ass is a killer!

"You right Re, but can I have some remorse?"

I felt bad for my boo. Clearly, she wasn't meant to be a killer.

"Ju, what would possess y'all to hit a bank? Keep that shit one hundred. You been lying to me for a minute, just thought I would let you know. She looked back at ReRe for support.

Poohman jumped in, "Don't look back here! Re's ass in deep shit, too!"

So for the next thirty minutes she told me how they were getting their dough around the hood. What she told me next shocked the fuck out of me. She told me that they hit that garage on Marquette.

"That was y'all? That was y'all, what?" I hit the steering wheel hard as fuck, scaring the fuck out of her. "Do you fucking know the bullshit that's about to come your way? Our way? Them niggas that was at the bank; that was they money y'all took, Ju!"

I couldn't believe this shit. "I grew up with them. They're some killers too. They're going to beat the streets until they find out what they wanna know." I didn't want to scare her, but it was the truth. We were about to go to war with Big Moe.

"Jaw, I'm not scared."

At that moment, I wanted to slap the shit outta her. She knew it too!

"It ain't about being scared. It's about being smart. They hit banks for a living. They kill for a living. How y'all hit the same bank at the same time was crazy, but damn Ju, you killed one of them and took they money! Twice! They coming!"

I looked at Poohman and said, "I know Big Moe grabbed those tapes!"

45 Minutes Later

We finally got back to my crib. "Poohman, grab one of these bags, my nigga."

"Tell Little Miss *Set It Off*, to do it!"

E and Tiki waited for us on the porch. "Damn, took y'all long enough."

Once we got in the crib, we got down to business counting that money. Four hours, two blunts, and three pizzas later, we were finally finished. All I could say was, "Damn shawty, y'all came the fuck up!"

We counted $803,517.00.

Meanwhile On the Other Side of Town

JR

I can't believe my brothers gone. He was all I had left. I keep playing that scene over in my head. How did they hit our lick? I blame Big Moe's ass. He should have had his information right. That was his setup. I'm trying to also figure out why Jaw was there. I know him a mile away. Was he in on that shit? Who were the bitches that were with him?

Who was that other cat? Why would Jaw have anything to do with killing Boogie?

"Tutu, come ere."

She walked in the room and gave me a hug. I pushed her ass back. "Bitch, fuck all that sentimental shit! Did you find out who Dirty E was?"

"Yeah."

I was waiting for her to finish. "And?"

"E is a girl and she hangs with three other girls name JuJu, Tiki, and ReRe."

I got up and grabbed my car keys. I had a few moves to make. I grabbed my .45 off the dresser and walked towards Tutu. "Maybe in the next lifetime you'll be a better bitch!" Before she could say shit else.

BOOM!

I shot that hoe in her lying ass mouth. She fell to the floor.

BOOM!

I shot her in the head for good measures. "Dirty Bitch!"

Big Moe

I done watched this tape over and over again trying to figure out who these motha fuckers are. The two we first ran up on in the bank were bitches. On the low, that was some gangsta ass shit. I can admit, but my pride won't let that go. Twice I've been beat for my money. Hell naw, I'm killing somebody. Right now, I'm too stressed to think. I need some pussy.

"Hello."

"What up with it?"

"Where you at?"

"At the crib chilling. Why? You trying to come break a bitch off?"

"Hell yeah. That's music to my ears."

"8415 South Marquette."

"I'm on the way."

Auntie Boo

Let me jump up and hit this shower real quick. It's been awhile since I've had some. I'm on no layup shit though. He can hit this pussy and be on his merry little way. As soon as I hit the shower, my phone rings. I looked at the caller ID and started to not answer.

"Hello."

"Auntie, I'm trying to come holla at you ASAP."

"Damn, you can't wait? I'm trying to get some."

"What I gotta say is better than some dick."

Now he's got my attention. "Better than dick, huh?"

"Hell yeah! All I'mma say is, that Ju and her little besties done set some shit off, and me and Poohman accidently helped them."

"Bring ya ass, now!"

"It's me, Poohman, Ju, and ReRe."

"Hurry up!"

Lil Mama

"Hey hoe! What you doing?"

"I think ya niece trying to be just like you when she grow up."

"Fuck you talking about? Spit that shit out!"

"All I'mma say over this phone is *Set It Off*!"

"OMG! NEVER!"

"Come through. They on their way here."

"I'm on the way."

JR

I've been all over the Eastside looking for these hoes that they call the *Eastside Crazy Crew*. From what I was told, these little bitches have been on a robbing spree. If these are the same hoes that hit the garage and that bank, I'mma enjoy killing they asses.

"Big Moe, where you at? Meet me somewhere."

"What's good nigga? I'm about to splash in some pussy."

"I found out who hit the spot over East."

"Oh yeah?"

"Yeah, and get this, they the same hoes that hit the bank."

"Hoes?"

"Yeah nigga, you heard me right, some hoes."

"Meet me at my little friends crib. 8415 Marquette."

"I'm right around the way."

E

I've been on turn up mode all day. We came up big time. I'm not even going to lie, that lick was fun as shit, boy! My besties are some gangstas! JuJu surprised the fuck out of me. I knew that she had a little gangsta up in her, but damn. She did that! We do need to sit down and figure out our next three moves. Tiki and I have been chilling downtown doing some light shopping. LJ and Poohman got Thelma and Louise on lock. I'm no hater, but we all need to talk.

"What yo ass over there thinking about?" Tiki brought me from my thoughts.

"Shit, we need to get up with Ju and Re. Call em."

She answered on the first ring. "Hey, what you up to?"

"Where you at, killa?"

"Don't call me that, bitch!"

"You better watch that bitch word, hoe. I'm a grown ass man."

"Yeah, you wish."

"Well, my dick say otherwise."

"Ugh, E! You nasty!

"What?"

"Where you at?"

"On the way to Boo's."

"ReRe with you?"

"Yeah, why?"

"We need to meet up ASAP and talk about a few things."

BEEP!

"Hold on Ju, my other line beeping." I clicked over. "Yo?"

"Dirty, some nigga riding around here in a tan Impala, paying motha fuckers for information about E.S.C."

"Word? Who talking?"

"You gon be mad, but fuck him. It'sLil Man."

"Damn! Alright my nigga thanks for the info."

I clicked back over mad as hell. "You still there?"

"I was about to hang up, shit! Got a bitch on hold like that!"

"Man, shut up. I'll meet y'all at Boo's."

Auntie Boo 17

Wonder why I don't have a verse on my page? I'm old school. Real G's don't need no introduction. Feel me? Damn, I need a beer! Let me call Jaw before he gets here.

"Yo?"

"Nephew, you'll stop and grab me a few beers? I'm about to throw a few steaks on the grill since y'all coming. My company just called and said he's bringing his cousin. So, I might as well, fill y'all asses."

"Who's yo company?"

"Nobody you know, nosey ass. Hurry up!"

"Alright, whatever!"

Lil Ma

Damn, I need to go see Pete real quick. I need to see if he found out what I was looking for. I hit Boo up to let her know I'mma be a few minutes late. "Boo, I gotta run by to see Pete real quick."

"Bitch, who you looking for?"

"Yo ass so damn nosey. I'll see you in a minute."

"I got some steaks on the grill. My new little tender is bringing his cousin."

"Lil tender? Bitch, how old is this little nigga and his cousin? I don't date kids."

"Fuck you hoe. I got him by like six years, but so what. Bring yo ass."

"Here you go with this blind date shit. I'm on my way. Bitch, if he got his pants sagging off his ass and he calls me shawty, I'm leaving."

Big Moe

"A, I'm outside baby."

"The doors open. Come up."

"I'm hungry. You gon whip a nigga up something?"

"I got some steaks on the grill. My nephew and his little friends are stopping by too. I called my little sister to keep your cousin company. That cool?"

"Yeah, I'm walking up the stairs."

LJ

"Poohman, grab them beers out the trunk."

"Nigga, what's wrong with yo hands?"

"You an ol' lazy bastard."

"So what, pussy. Yo mama like it."

"I'mma tell her you said that shit too."

"What? Na, I'm just playing. I got em."

"Thought so."

That nigga doesn't want problems with my mom Dukes, AKA Heidi D. Back in the days, mom Dukes and my Auntie Boo ran the projects. Which one? Shit, all of em'. My Auntie Boo was a beast on the drug game. She slung the pistols even harder.

My mom Dukes straight just knocked niggas out. Literally! My daddy saw a few stars fucking with her crazy ass. So Poohman already knows that shes bout that life.

"Auntie, we downstairs."

As we head to the stairs, this little chick from across the street calls JuJu. "Hey Ju, let me put a bug in your ear."

She turns to look at me. "Go head, but hurry up baby. It's about to rain."

As she begins to cross the street, I get this fucked up feeling in the pit of my stomach. I look at Poohman who's also looking at me. I don't even have to say shit. He knows me too well.

"What Jaw? We got beef?"

I shake my head. "Na, my nigga. Something just don't feel right."

JR

As I'm riding down Marquette looking for the address that my cousin gave me, I see Jaw,

Poohman, and two familiar looking bitches walking towards the house that I'm looking for. I haven't even hit Jaw up since that shit went down. Fuck it! My brother dies by the hands of a bitch that you leave with. That makes him just as guilty as her in my book.

"Fuck are they doing over here?"

I pick my phone up and hit my cousin.

Big Moe

"Yo cuz, where you at?"

"I'm a few houses away from where you at."

"Then come on up. You tripping. My little shawty got some steaks on the grill."

"How well you know this bitch?"

"Nigga, fuck the riddles. Spit that shit out."

"You know I was saying that I found out who hit both licks."

"Right. Who told you?"

"Tutu told me, right before I shot her grimy ass. I told you that those niggas at the bank looked familiar."

"Who you thought they was?"

"Jaw and Poohman."

"The little niggas you went to school with?"

"Yeah."

"So what up?"

"They asses walking up the stairs to where you at."

"FUCK YOU JUST SAY?" I had to catch my tone.

"You good boo?" I looked at shawty with pure hatred, but I knew I had to keep it cool.

"Yeah ma, I'm cool."

After she walked back into the kitchen, I put my plan into motion. "JR wait a few minutes and then come up. Were Poohman and Jaw alone?"

"I saw two bitches with them, but now it's only one."

"Wait about ten minutes and then come up."

I'm on fucking fire. Is the hoe trying to set me up? See, this is why I don't trust hoes now.

KNOCK! KNOCK!

"Ramon, can you open the door?"

JuJu

"What up, Katari?"

"Bitch, where you been? I been trying to get a hold of you for two weeks now."

"I been booked up. What's up?"

"I see. I asked Tyesha where you were. Anyway, bitch shit just got real out here."

"Well don't keep me in suspense."

"First, rumor has it that you and yo crew killed Pancho."

My mouth almost hit the ground. "Who the fuck lying like that?"

"Lil Man said y'all killed his brother and ain't nobody heard from his sister, Tutu."

"I don't even know a Tutu and his little ass better quit lying like that before I get Woodie to fuck his little ass up."

"That ain't even the half. Some nigga been riding around the hood in a tan Impala looking for some nigga named, Dirty E."

"What he look like?"

"I haven't seen him, but I know he paid Lil Man and now he knows that E is a girl. I also know who y'all is too."

"E, gon get that little shit."

"Just be careful. You know you my boo thang."

"Thanks boo." I picked up the phone to call Jaw. No answer! Fuck it. He's just going to have to come with me to fuck Lil Man up real quick. As I start walking back across the street towards the house, I could feel the hairs on the back of my neck stand up.

"What's that all about?" I say to no one in particular. As I reach the top of the stairs, I don't hear shit. "They must be on the back porch."

I turn the knob to enter Boo's apartment, and out of nowhere, I feel a gun being pressed to my back. "Bitch, I'mma kill you just like you killed my brother!"

I could have pissed myself right then and there. I tried to turn around, but he pushed me through the door. What I saw next, brought me to my knees. Jaw and Poohman laying unconscious. Boo and my besties were all tied up on their knees with duct tape over their mouths. I was so into my conversation with my girl outside that I didn't even see E and Tiki pull up.

Damn, out of all the shit I've done in my life, I never thought that it would end like this. As I look into the eyes of my besties, I see no fear. We came up together, got money together, cried together, killed together, and shit, I guess it looks like we're bout to lay it down together. We had a great run together. We shook this motha fuckingg city up like dice. For real!

Coming up, all we had was each other. We didn't give a fuck about nobody because nobody gave a fuck about us. We rode hard in these streets, burning a lot of motha fuckers in the process. What? We E.S.C., Eastside Crazy! You better know it.

We fucked up though. We got comfortable, started sleeping on the enemies and they swarmed on our asses like killer bees. As I stand here ready to meet my maker, I can't help but wonder, *did I choose the wrong career path*? Hearing the hammer cock back on the gun that I'm sure would end our lives; I can't help but see my life flash before my eyes. The beginning was bad, but this shit right here, my nigga is death… Literally!

Lil Mama

Why the fuck isn't nobody answering their phones? Agghh! This shit is pissing me off. I got some words for Boo's ass. I love my sister, but she's been keeping shit from me. Call me paranoid if you want, but I had Pete watching her ass. She's back in the game and I'm mad about it. I thought that time was enough to shut her ass down. It's dangerous and she's got enemies that she don't even know about.

From what Pete said, the nigga that told on her is sniffing around town trying to get the drop on her. Why is he looking for her now? I don't know, but it's not good.

"Boo, pick up the phone. I'm on my way over. Pete told me some shit. I'mma kill yo ass, just so you know."

JR

"Bitch, I'mma kill every last one of these motha fuckers and you're going to watch me do it. You made me watch my brother die, so I'mma gladly return the favor."

I looked around the room at each and every face. Sure enough, these are the little bastards that hit up my garage, and the bank in Indiana.

"Big Moe, we got stained by some fucking kids. Where the fuck our money at from the garage and the bank?"

I snatched the tape off of the stud broad's mouth. "Talk pussy!"

This little bitch looked up at me, hawked, and spit in my face. "Fuck you, nigga!"

The nerve of this bitch ass nigga. "OH YEAH?"

WHACK!

I punched that bitch in her mouth so hard that my knuckles bust. "You gon be the first one I torture and kill."

I turned my attention to this pretty ass bitch with emerald green eyes. I remember those eyes. No lie; she was the one that upped that AK-47 on us at the bank. The way she shot ol' girl in the head without hesitation, I knew not to underestimate her. She was a killer. I snatched the tape from her mouth.

"I know those eyes. You the bitch from the bank with the AK."

She just looked at me. The look she gave me sent shivers down my spine. "Oh, you think you tough?"

Still no answer.

"Okay, have it your way."

I walked over to where I had knocked Poohman's ass out.

"Where that money?"

Her eyes shot daggers at me. Guaranteed, if she could get to me, she'd try to kill me. I like a gangsta ass bitch. "I'mma come back to you. We got all day, but this nigga I don't need."

I pointed the gun at Poohman's stomach.

BOOM!

"POOHMAN! NOOOOOO!"

"Oh, you do talk."

ReRe

All I know is, one minute we were all laughing, walking up the stairs and the next thing I know, we had a big ass gun pointed at our faces.

"Get the fuck on the ground!"

"What the fuck?"

"Bitch, shut the fuck up!"

Then out of nowhere, WHACK! WHACK!

This crazy ass nigga knocked Poohman and Jaw out cold. I'm mad that I left my pistol in the car. He snatches me in the crib and that's when I see Boo tied up on the floor.

"Lay down, hoe!"

Damn, I'm about to die like this? I hope Ju don't come up here. I want my bestie to live her life to the fullest. My life has been fucked up since birth. I don't have a soul. I don't have shit, really. I'm used up. That's why I haven't let Poohman sex me. I'm too scared that he won't like it, because my daddy used me up.

Oh God! I hear people coming up the stairs. Shit, think! Fuck! It's E and Tiki. I can't call out to them because I don't want to get shot. Shit, I'm about to die anyway. As I got up enough air in my lungs to scream past this tape on my mouth, I guess the dude saw me make that effort. This grimy motha fucker hit me so hard in my stomach that I saw stars.

"UGHH!"

"E, don't," was all I got out before everything went black.

E

"Man, I'm hungrier than that thing." Tiki looked at me like, what's new. "Tiki, call one of them hoes and tell them we are around the corner."

She picked up her phone. "Neither one of their asses are answering the phone. Probably all boo loving and shit."

"Let me find out, you jealous." She looked at me as if I was crazy.

"You know better."

We hit Marquette and found a parking spot. "They're here because there go Jaw's Charger."

To be honest, the whole scene didn't feel right to me. As we made our way up the stairs, I felt funny as shit.

"E, what the hell? Why you looking like you smell a shitty diaper?"

"I don't know, Tiki. I don't feel right."

"Quit smoking all that weed, hoe."

"Whatever!"

We get to the top of the stairs and I swear it is quiet as hell. I went to reach for the doorknob when all of a sudden, the door flies open.

"What's good, Dirty E?"

Lil Mama

I can't believe that nobody's answering their phones. I need to talk to Boo.

"Fuck!" I hit the steering wheel while being caught at a red light. I look up to see this old ass lady mean mugging me.

"What the fuck you looking at, Granny? Mind your business, ol' nosey bitch!"

Yes, I was that mad. As I pulled up to her crib, there were no parking spots. "Are you serious?"

I finally find one a few houses down. As soon as I get out, I see my niece's little friend Katari running towards me.

"Girl, why you looking like somebody just slapped the shit outta you?"

"You need to get up there, now! I heard a shot and I heard somebody scream!"

"WHAT?"

"I saw this nigga creep up there after JuJu left from over here. I been calling, but she ain't answering."

"FUCK!

I'm on parole. I don't need this shit. I ran back to my car and popped my trunk. I grabbed my gun and checked the chamber. What? Better safe than sorry. This the Eastside of Chicago. These niggas don't discriminate. Parole or not, I stay strapped and for future references, don't bring your ass over here without one.

I hit the gangway and quietly crept up the back stairs. As I make my way to the top of the stairs, I could hear voices coming from the kitchen area.

"Big Moe, don't kill em yet. We need that money, nigga."

"Fuck all that. Let's shoot these motha fuckers and be done with it. We can hit another spot. I'mma start with that bitch Boo since she wanna set niggas up."

Kill Boo? Shoot WHO? Not my sister. Okay think! Before I could come up with anything, all hell broke loose.

JuJu

I'mma be fucked up for life after this shit. I'm not even worried about me. I feel bad for my bestie. She can't do shit, but watch Poohman bleed to death. I'm hurting more because it's been years since I saw ReRe cry. She's just over there rocking back and forth and the tears and just flowing. When we finally made eye contact, all hell broke loose!

ReRe

I can't believe this pussy ass nigga, shot my man. If we're going to die, it won't be like this. I see JuJu looking at me and I can't help but to cry harder. She might think it's because of Poohman being shot, but it isn't. I got this blade in my hands and I'm slowly cutting away at the tape. Thing is, the tape isn't the only thing I'm cutting. I'm fucking my damn wrists up. That's why I'm crying. This shit hurt!

I block the pain because I'm almost there. POP! I snapped the tape in half. Now it's on! I crawled over to where Jaw and Poohman laid and snatched the tape off of their mouths.

"Jaw, where --."

He cut me off. "My auntie got that Choppa under the couch. Hurry up so I can get him to the hospital."

I looked towards the kitchen to see where they were. I hurried up and cut Jaw loose.

"Aww shit! Here they come!"

Jaw looked at me with murder all in his eyes. "Chop their ass down!"

That's all I needed to hear. I put my back against the wall and waited. That nigga, JR was the first to hit the corner. "Talk that shit now!"

He looked at me and said some real shit. "Bitch, I been ready!"

I went to pull the trigger. CLICK! CLICK!

He smiled at me. "I guess God ain't ready for me."

WHACK! He punched me so hard in my face that I went flying backwards dropping the gun. After that, he was all over me. I can throw these paws with the best of them, but this nigga was possessed. As we rolled around on the floor, I could see Jaw and JuJu fighting Big Moe.

E, Tiki, and Boo were still tied up. I could see my baby still laying on the floor clutching his stomach. That gave me some type of energy. I grabbed this nigga's balls and tried to pull them the fuck off.

"Yeah bitch, I like that freaky shit!"

That must have gave him a burst of energy because he started hitting me harder and faster. I was on the verge of blacking out when I hear; POP! POP! POP!

He falls on top of me. "What? Get him off of me!" I had no strength left after fighting this clown. I'm trying to push him off of me, but he is dead weight for real. Who the fuck shot him? I saw Lil Mama pull him one-way so that I could slide from up under him the other way.

"Y'all alright? Where Big Moe, Jaw?"

Jaw's ass was still breathing hard. "That nigga ran out the front door after he heard the shots."

I ran over to where Poohman was lying. "Baby, let me see your wound."

I lift his shirt up and I see a hole the size of a dime. I didn't see blood.

"Shit Jaw! We gotta get him to the hospital. He's bleeding internally."

Lil Man

On my mama, I'mma kill every last one of them pussy ass motha fuckers. I just got a call from my mama. They just found my sister dead in her apartment. Bad enough, I just lost my brother. He took care of me. He always made sure I had the best video games and the newest Jordan's. I can't believe Dirty E and those three bitches crossed him like that. I got something for their asses. Watch!

Lil Mama

These last few days been crazy. After that shit that happened at Boo's crib, I've been on full alert. Poohman in critical condition. JuJu been at the hospital with Jaw. I'mma have a talk with all their little asses when I get the time. See, I had Pete watching their little asses too! They're really out here doing the most. Robbing drug dealers and they just hit a bank. What type of shit is this? I mean, here I am trying to stay on the right path. My sister's back in the drug game. My niece and her little besties making power moves and shit. It almost makes me want to... Hell naw! Fuck that! Eight years was long enough. But damn, that little $250,000.00 I got stashed isn't going to last long.

RING! RING!

"What up sis?"

"Come pick me up. We need to talk."

Auntie Boo

I'mma kill these fucking kids! I don't know what the hell they got us into. Then this nigga Ramon or Big Moe, whatever his name is. I'mma personally kill that bitch when I catch up with him. One minute I'm grilling steaks and having a decent conversation, and the next thing you know, I'm being hit over the head with a gun. What part of the game is that?

My murder game is official. Niggas respect my name, alone. Apparently, my nephew and his friends have been real busy. It was almost impossible trying to convince the police that somebody tried to run up in my crib. Had Poohman not been shot, we'd all be in jail for that nigga's body. Lil Mama got ghost before they even came.

After that, Jaw told me some shit that had me stuck on stupid. First, he had been moving weight since he was fifteen and he was doing it under Heidi's and my nose. Second, JuJu and her little besties not only robbed Big Moe for $350,000.00, but they also robbed a bank that Big Moe and his boys were trying to rob at the same damn time!

Then Poohman and Jaw accidently helped, adding themselves to Big Moe's murder list. Small world! Who knew that I would end up talking to the same Big Moe? I just called Lil Mama and told her to come get me. I was out of the game for a minute when I got out the FEDS. That nine to five shit just wasn't for me. So I shut up my dude, and just kind of, you know… Got back down!

I'm extra paranoid though. Niggas telling like crazy. I can't give these people no more of my life, but this is the life. I missed the power that I had over Chicago. I was that bitch. Fuck that. I am that bitch! I think Lil Mama and I could guide these little go-getters the way that we got around us.

I thought their little asses were some squares, but they fooled the shit outta me. I'm down to take over this city one more time. For good! I see it in Lil Mama's eyes. She has some gas left in her tank. She's a fool with them pistols, too. We got our whole squad already.

KNOCK! KNOCK!

"I hate when you knock, Lil Mama." I walked towards the door and swung it open. "Bitch, you could have --."

My words got caught in my throat when I saw who was standing before me. My mentor, my friend. The man that taught me the game stood before me with a gun pointed at my head.

"I know you saw me."

I knew exactly what he was talking about. A while ago, I got up with him to discuss some business. He was too jittery for my liking so I told him that I had shit to do. I jumped in my whip and peeled off. Something told me to double back. Sure enough, this snake ass nigga hopped in a white Impala with the FEDS.

He called me for three days straight. I had no words for him. Next thing you know, I'm being indicted for a whole rack of shit. I knew better than to take that shit to trial. I pleaded out and ended up with six years. Needless to say, his ass disappeared. I never told the guys about his role in bringing me down. I guess he'd finish me off so I'd take his secret to the grave.

Now he's standing here with murder all in his eyes.

"I didn't tell nobody; just so you know."

He looked at me with tears in his eyes. A look I never saw. I knew then that I was about to die.

"You will take that to your grave!"

I just had to ask. "Why did you do me like that? BOOM!

*"I'm slipping, I'm falling, I can't get up
I'm slipping, I'm falling, I can't get up
I'm slipping, I'm falling, I got to get up
get back on my feet so I can tear shit up!"*

Big Moe 18

"Hello."

"Yo, this Big Moe. Where you at? I fucking need you right now!"

"What's wrong?"

"Bitch, just get here."

"I got yo bitch! Where's Junior? Hello! Where the fuck is my brother, Ramone?"

"It wasn't my fault."

CLICK!

FUCK! I'll find another ride. I can't believe this shit. I thought that bitch Boo was official. Everything is all fucked up now. How did we get caught slipping? Damn! Junior and Boogie both are gone. I'm low on my stash. Those little motha fuckers took all our bread. I need to lay low and regroup.

I'm too fucking scared to drive so I start walking towards 87th street to the bus stop when somebody calls me.

"A, wait up."

I turned around about to shoot this motha fucker when I see it's a fucking kid.

"Fuck you want, little nigga?"

"I just saw you run up outta that crib on 84th."

I start looking around because I'm about to snatch this little bastard in one of these gangways and shoot his ass. He saw my actions and he put his hands up.

"Whoa homie! I am not the law. I just wanna know, did you kill them four bitches."

I stared at him as if he was fucking crazy. "What four bitches?"

"Them four bitches that killed my brother when they stole that money outta that garage."

"Who the fuck are you?"

This little fucker had heart. He poked his chest out and tilted his head to the side. "My name is Lil Man. If you didn't kill em'; I wanted to!"

"You want to?"

"Hell yeah! They killed my brother!"

I think I could use this little motha fucker as bait.

"How old are you?"

"I'll be fourteen in three weeks. I know where they hang at. I just need a pistol."

I thought about it for a few more seconds. "Alright. I might be able to help you out."

"Bet!"

*"Bad boys, bad boys, whatcha gonna do
whatcha gonna do when they come for you?
Bad boys, bad boys, whatcha gonna do
whatcha gonna do when they come for you?"*

Detective Malone 19

"**O**kay, shut the hell up so I can properly brief y'all on what our next assignment is. This will be operation E.S.C." I looked around the room to see if I had everyone's attention.

"My informant has briefed me, so now I can fill you all in. In the past two months, there have been three murders, several robberies, and a series of other crimes that are now on my radar. Rumor has it; these four little perps have been running around robbing and murdering people. I have a big problem with that. I could give a rat's ass if they kill each other. Less work for us."

I could hear a few chuckles in the room.

"The problem is that they are supposedly responsible for the double homicide in that bank robbery in Hammond, Indiana. Now I got the chief sniffing up my ass and I don't like that. My ass is off limits!"

A rookie by the name of House spoke up, "Boss, ain't Indiana out of our jurisdiction?"

"Yeah, but we are gonna do what we can to help them out and keep the chief far away from my ass. Besides those little bastards are from our district. Now my informant says that she knows the perps really well. They are believed to be armed and dangerous."

Just as I was finishing up my speech, the dispatcher called.

"All units available, we have a possible 187 in progress. Please respond to 8415 South Marquette. Neighbors have reported shots fired."

House was the first to speak, "Boss, ain't that the house that had that shootout a few days ago?"

"Yeah, and it's your time to show me what you got, rookie!"

I dismissed the officers and made my way to my office for some privacy.

"Hello, this is Malone. Did you give him the address? Okay. Don't do shit until you hear from me. Bitch listen to me. Shut the fuck up then. I'll pay you when I know the job is done."

I sat down at my desk and I had to shake my damn head. All my life, I wanted to be a cop. You know the 'protect and serve' kind of cop. I worked my ass off as a rookie. Then I became a Lieutenant and then a Homicide Detective. I followed the rules and what do I get in return? A bunch of ungrateful motherfuckers in this city. The harder I work, the more I see how ungrateful my own department can be. The pay is on a check-to-check basis. I can't live like that, so I turned to the dark side.

My best informant was found dead in a garage a few weeks ago. That shit really hurt my pockets. Now I'm dealing with his woman. She claims to have solid information on the Eastside Crazy Crew.

I want that money they stole from Pancho. I'm not going to stop until I body their little asses.

I got up from my desk ready to respond to the Marquette call when my phone rings.

"Hello."

"Boss, you need to get over here now!"

"I'm on my way. What's wrong?"

"You'll never believe who's on the stretcher fighting for her life!"

"Who dammit?"

"Just get here, Boss! If she makes it, all hell is gonna break loose!"

"Fuck!"

"Let a nigga try me, try me
I'mma kill his whole mafucking family
and I ain't playing with nobody
fuck around and I'mma catch a body!"

Lil Mama 20

"**H**i, you've reached Boo. Leave a message."

"Bitch, how you going to tell me to come get you and now you not answering the phone." I hung up mad as fuck! I hate that shit! I got so many thoughts running through my head right now. I know that she's about to tell me that she's back in the game. Ugggh! I'm frustrated. When she was on, it was love. We didn't have to worry about money, but fuck I'm on parole. Federal parole at that.

"What the fuck?" I pulled up on the block and there were police and ambulances everywhere. I tried to find a parking spot when I hear my name. "Lil Mama, get out! Get out!" I see my niece's friend running up to my car. "What the hell is going on?"

She's breathing so hard that I can barely understand her. "Calm down! Now tell me what's wrong!"

"Somebody shot Boo!"

That's all she got out of her mouth before I pushed her little ass out my way and took off running full speed up the block. I made it to her yard before a police officer grabbed me. "Ma'am, you can't go in there."

"Let me go! That's my sister's house!"

He wasn't letting up so that shit sent me through the roof. "LET ME THE FUCK GO! WHERE'S MY SISTER?" I'm screaming at the top of my lungs when the paramedics bring my sister out on a stretcher.

"BOO? BOO, WHO DID THIS? SIS, WAKE UP PLEASEEEE!"

My pleas went on deaf ears because she wasn't responding. "Let me go, please! She fucking need me!" Now I'm jumping up and down acting a damn fool because this pussy ass police won't let me go.

"Ma'am, I'mma cuff you if you don't calm down!"

I let them load her up into the ambulance. "A, Woodie get my car and follow the ambulance!" I got ready to try to get in the ambulance when the paramedic grabbed me. "Let me go! I'm riding with my sister!"

He looked down and then back at me. "Ma'am, she's nonresponsive."

I'm having a hard time understanding what he's saying. "She needs me! Let me ride with her, please?" The last thing I heard before I saw black was, "I'm sorry, but she's gonna be DOA."

LJ

Man, shit's been crazy this whole summer. Within two months, I met a chick; fell in love with her, accidently helped her and her besties rob a bank, and witnessed a few murders. The little chick and her besties came up in a major way. I haven't seen a chick more about that life, but man Joe, with the good came the bad. My best friend is in the hospital fighting for his life. We got this crazy ass nigga, Big Moe on the prowl. Both of his cousins are dead because of somebody in our crew.

I need my homie to get right. We got this money to make. We also need to find Big Moe and send his ass on a one-way ticket to hell. My Auntie Boo blessed us with her Jamaican connect. That's a boss bitch, for real! Man, I swear that lady is untouchable. With her back in the game, I'm sure we're about to hit that millionaire status sooner than later. I'm really trying to make enough dough so my boo Ju can relax and finish school. I don't want her out here in these streets doing all this crazy shit.

I got a feeling that her little ass got turned out to this bullshit. It doesn't help when her three best friends are all about that life. I have never seen three young chicks that go so hard. Sadly, murder is a part of that equation.

When I saw ReRe shoot that lady at the bank, I was stuck. But, what took the icing on the cake was when my girl popped Boogie's ass with no hesitation. I've been in the streets for a minute and I have never level a nigga down. I never had to. I know for a fact that I'mma pop Big Moe's ass.

"Excuse me Sir; your friend wants to see you."

"Thank you."

I walk back to Poohman's room happy to see my boy sitting up on his own. That bullet to the stomach fucked him up. It hit a few organs and now it's logged in his back a few inches from his spinal cord.

"What it do?"

"Bro, she gone," he said crying.

I looked at his ass as if he was on fire. I have never seen Poohman cry. I instantly started crying. "Who's gone?" I shoulda sat down had I known what he was about to say. Maybe I wouldn't have hurt myself because what he said brought me to my knees, hard!

"Auntie Boo! He shot her! She's gone, Jaw!"

"My Besties, the Take Over"
COMING SOON!

New Release

<u>48 Hours To Die: An Anthony Stone Novel by</u>

<u>Silk White</u>

Free E-Books From

Good2go Publishing

Limited Time Only

The Serial Cheater PT 1 By Silk White

He Loves Me, He Loves You Not By Mychea

Tears Of A Hustler PT 1 By Silk White

Slumped PT 1 By Jason Brent

My Boyfriend's Wife PT 1 By Mychea

The Panty Ripper PT 1 By Reality Way E-Book

Books by Good2Go Authors on Our Bookshelf

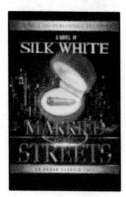  

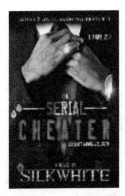

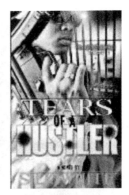

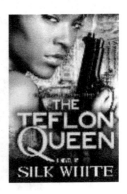

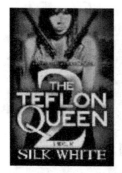

Good2Go Films Presents

CPSIA information can be obtained at www.ICGtesting.com
Printed in the USA
LVOW04s1457200515

439231LV00014B/684/P

9 780990 869450

To order books, please fill out the order form below:

To order films please go to **www.good2gofilms.com**

Name:_____

Address:_____

City: _____ State: _____ Zip Code: _____

Phone:_____

Email:_____

Method of Payment: Check   VISA   MASTERCARD

Credit Card#:_____

Name as it appears on card: _____

Signature: _____

Item Name	Price	Qty	Amount
48 Hours to Die – Silk White	$14.99		
Flipping Numbers – Ernest Morris	$14.99		
He Loves Me, He Loves You Not - Mychea	$14.99		
He Loves Me, He Loves You Not 2 - Mychea	$14.99		
He Loves Me, He Loves You Not 3 - Mychea	$14.99		
Married To Da Streets – Silk White	$14.99		
My Boyfriend's Wife - Mychea	$14.99		
Never Be The Same – Silk White	$14.99		
Stranded – Silk White	$14.99		
Slumped – Jason Brent	$14.99		
Tears of a Hustler - Silk White	$14.99		
Tears of a Hustler 2 - Silk White	$14.99		
Tears of a Hustler 3 - Silk White	$14.99		
Tears of a Hustler 4- Silk White	$14.99		
Tears of a Hustler 5 – Silk White	$14.99		
Tears of a Hustler 6 – Silk White	$14.99		
The Panty Ripper - Reality Way	$14.99		
The Panty Ripper 2 – Reality Way	$14.99		
The Teflon Queen – Silk White	$14.99		
The Teflon Queen 2 – Silk White	$14.99		
The Teflon Queen 3 – Silk White	$14.99		
The Teflon Queen 4 – Silk White	$14.99		
Time Is Money - Silk White	$14.99		
Young Goonz – Reality Way	$14.99		
Subtotal:			
Tax:			
Shipping (Free) U.S. Media Mail:			
Total:			

Make Checks Payable To: Good2Go Publishing - 7311 W Glass Lane, Laveen, AZ 85339